POMERANIAN PUZZLE

A SMALL TOWN COZY MYSTERY

MOLLY MAPLE

MARY E. TWOMEY, LLC

POMERANIAN PUZZLE

Book One in the Apple Blossom Bay Series

By

Molly Maple

COPYRIGHT

DEDICATION

To Melissa Storm,

Who came to me like an angel in a storm and gave me the best dog in the world.

When Hannah Hart moves to the small town of Apple Blossom Bay to look after her eccentric aunt, she doesn't expect the first thing she finds to be a murder.

Apple Blossom Bay is known for its fresh seafood and peaceful beaches, so when Hannah uncovers a dead body on her first day in town, she doesn't know who to trust. While her aunt has a questionable alibi, every claim out of her mouth is wilder than the last. The only friend Hannah can rely on is the stray dog who was found at the scene of the crime.

With a sweet toy Pomeranian in need of a new home, and Hannah in need of a friend she can trust, the two team up to figure out who could possibly have murdered a resident of Apple Blossom Bay. If she doesn't get to the bottom of who murdered Barb, Hannah is positive she will be on next on the killer's list.

"Pomeranian Puzzle" is an inclusive cozy mystery filled with layered clues and quirky moments, written by Molly Maple, which is a pen name for a USA Today bestselling author.

FIRST DAY IN APPLE BLOSSOM BAY

The air feels different in Apple Blossom Bay. It's not just the smack of the ocean infiltrating my freckled nose and the pores on my face; there's a depth to the air that somehow makes my whole body feel light.

I can't remember the last time I felt a lightness in my spirit, much less my body.

The drive from Chicago to Apple Blossom Bay took approximately seven million hours in my beat-up old red sedan, which is only a slight exaggeration. While the actual drive didn't take quite that long, the road to get me to come back to the town where my aunt lives has been two decades too many.

With an eviction notice looming and my mom hinting for the fiftieth time that my aunt could use some help around her house, since she's getting on in years, I packed up my things and drove across the country to a town so small, my GPS practically quirked its eyebrow at me when I typed in the new address.

Admitting defeat that my job at the gas station wouldn't and couldn't pay my bills is a shame I have carried through every rest stop along the way. The only thing I will miss back home is the stray dog who came sniffing around the gas station around noon every day, begging for treats, which I happily baked for him.

I wonder if he misses me, and who will give him treats now that I'm gone.

My parents warned me that living on my own was a bad idea. They wanted me to get a desk job that matched the degree they picked out for me. They said working at the gas station would be too tricky without my prosthetic hand, but that wasn't what slowed me down. It rarely is.

My rent increased and my hourly wage never climbed to match, so the gap between what came in and what went out grew wider and wider.

I hate that I failed. I hate that my parents were right.

I didn't know if I would be glad to be back in Apple Blossom Bay until I cross the city limits. Finally, the knot in my chest that I assumed would be permanent begins to loosen.

Maybe it's the pollution from the city air that never really lets you enjoy a full breath.

Maybe it's the lack of nature back home starkly contrasted with greenery so lush; it spoils you at first glance.

Whatever it is that fills my lungs with serenity now convinces me in a single breath that packing up my life in the city and moving across the country wasn't such a bad idea after all. In fact, it just might be the best thing that's happened to me in a long time.

At least, that's what I tell myself when I march up the driveway. I knock on the front door of the address from which my favorite aunt sends me a Christmas card every year.

I haven't seen my Aunt Em since I was a little girl. I hope she is still that magical person in my memory who brings joy easily to everyone she's near.

I should have stopped at a gas station on the way to splash some water on my face or something. I'm sure I look as road weary as I feel.

Though, maybe my aunt won't care that my strawberry blonde hair is knotted into a lopsided ponytail, and my gray shirt is wrinkled beyond repair. Hopefully she won't notice the coffee stain on the thigh of my jeans that I acquired during an unfortunate merging situation two states ago.

I'm not supposed to steer my car with my knee. I'm not supposed to do a lot of things.

My mom has a good many stories about how upsettingly absurd her sister has always been, so I don't know what to expect, or how nervous I should be.

All the way nervous, my adrenal system informs me, as it

always does when anything outside my normal routine rears its ugly head.

I do well with systems. With predictability. With order and routine. I stayed at the same job without a raise for all seven years of my adult life. Now here I am, twenty-five and starting over in a new place where I cannot predict a single thing.

My dad claims I am special needs, just because I was born without my right hand. He also tells his friends that I am bisexual, only he says it in a whisper, as if it's something strange.

My mom tells everyone who will listen that I have OCD, and that I live "an alternative lifestyle," simply because I like men and women.

I have no idea which labels I want to claim as mine.

Unhappy, my heart tells me, though I try not to listen.

Scared, my stomach tells me when thoughts of all the new things I will need to adjust to dawn on me.

I don't know where Aunt Em's bathroom is. I don't know if she wears shoes in the house. I don't know how she cleans her floors, or even what sort of floors she has inside. I don't know what size bed I'll be sleeping on, and therefore I don't know if the sheets I brought will fit. I don't know what my aunt likes to eat, or if she has dietary restrictions.

Sweat dampens my armpits and the crooks of my elbows, as it always does when my worry overtakes my sanity. I set down one of my suitcases on the porch, hoping my aunt likes me.

I tap the thumb on my left hand to my middle finger three times and take a deep breath.

I can do this. I can start over. People do it all the time.

When I press the doorbell, my eyes fall on a note taped to the door with my name on it.

DEAREST HANNAH GRAPEFRUIT,

I'M LOOKING AT HOUSES. MAKE YOURSELF AT HOME. I'LL BE BACK soon.

LOVE,

AUNT EMILY

I SMILE AT THE SILLY NICKNAME I'D LONG SINCE FORGOTTEN. Everyone called me Hannah Banana when I was a little girl, which I took issue with as a precocious child. Aunt Emily was the only one who listened to my fussing and started tacking a different fruit onto the end of my name, which I greatly appreciated.

I have a small collection of memories of my Aunt Em, but most of what I know has come from my mother—the older sibling who is constantly frustrated that her younger sister never quite learned to take the world and its expectations seriously.

Which is, coincidentally, the exact issue my mother has with me.

After I graduated with a business degree and no real plan on how to make a living with it, I was shunted into the same category to which my mother relegated my eccentric aunt. When Mom got word that Aunt Em might need help around the house, it was heavily "suggested" that I pack up and move across the country to be with the only other member of our family who was born without a serious edge and unbreakable drive.

I take in another cleansing breath, willing the ocean air to tell me I belong here.

To tell me I belong *anywhere*.

I tuck a stray strawberry blonde curl behind my ear and push open the heavy front door, timid in announcing my presence to the empty ranch home, as if it must know I am a stranger who doesn't belong here.

"I'm walking into the house," I sing awkwardly and most certainly off-key. Even though I am making up the tune as I go, it is obvious even to the owl-shaped ceramic cookie jar on the coffee table beside the lime green couch that I am tone deaf.

Hopefully the ceramic owl doesn't judge me too harshly.

The moment I set down my suitcase, my cell phone rings in my pocket. "Aunt Em? I'm here!" I sing once again, making myself wince with my lack of finesse when it comes to carrying a tune.

My aunt's deeper voice is foreign to my ears since we've only emailed a few times to set up the move. Other than that, I haven't had much contact with her since I was little.

"Oh, good! Say, drop off your things and come over to the address I'm texting you right now. I'm helping a couple look at houses. The next one on the list is cute! We're heading over there now."

I smirk at her enthusiasm. No one in my family back in the city gets excited about anything except achievements, so her joy is a welcome change.

It takes me all of five minutes to unload my things into her living room, and another five to pull into the driveway of the address she sent me. Though it feels as if I have been in the car for the better part of a century, my energy is renewed when I catch sight of my Aunt Em pulling up behind me on the sidewalk.

At least, I think it's her. It's been so long. When she gets out of her purple Jeep, I see flashes of the woman who took me sledding when my parents swore that I couldn't go outside, or I would catch a cold. My devious Aunt Em sneaked me out before the sun rose the next morning and took me sledding on a nearby hill.

I don't remember the Christmas presents I got when I was only four years old.

I don't recall my preschool teacher's name.

I couldn't guess at the kinds of treats I ate while the grownups were doing their important things.

But I still remember the glee I felt at the icy wind hitting my face when Aunt Em took me sledding for the first (and only) time in my life.

Before my awkward nature can take over my body and turn me into a wallflower, Aunt Em scoops me into a grand hug.

I can't remember the last time anyone hugged me. I'm not sure my memory stretches that far back. The sensation is heady. It's like being dunked underwater and dowsed in a warmth so acute; I can barely breathe through the onslaught of emotions.

"Oh, Hannah! It's so good to see you! Tell me everything about the trip. Make me feel like I was there." Then she pauses and shakes her head. "Tell me after the showing. Did your mother tell you that I'm a realtor now? Just got my license two months ago, and I daresay I'm not too bad at it. I do plenty of this," she informs me as she releases me from the hug so she can spread her arms to the left like a model on a game show.

I laugh at her energy, which happens to be contagious. After the monotony of the drive, I'm surprised anything perks me up.

My Aunt Em's smile stretches without hesitation or the

barest hint of mirth. She has olive skin, like my mother, and straight black hair that is swept into a ponytail to accentuate the supermodel-like angles of her jaw. She stands an inch over six feet tall—two inches taller than me —and has a slender frame similar to mine.

Only on my confident and stylish aunt, all those things come together to make her look like she is primed for a fashion show. She is clad in khaki shorts and a silky blue sleeveless blouse with flowing sleeves that bell down to mid-thigh. On me, the height and the bony nature of my body make me look like a marionette who's missing a string.

Aunt Em holds my shoulders, giving me a thorough once over. "My clients will be here any second. Tell me, do you still love to go sledding?"

I cast around at the spring weather, which sports bursts of greenery at every turn. "I haven't been since I went with you when I was a little girl, and I'm pretty sure nature isn't ready to take anybody sledding anytime soon." I smile at her energy, and the pretty hazel eyes that look like they have never been bogged down a day in their life.

She bats away my hesitation. "We can figure out a way around the snow. You leave that to me."

Aunt Em speaks with the confidence of a cartoon princess, certain the world will work itself out for a grand happily ever after.

She turns me to the quaint one-story house we are standing on the sidewalk in front of. "She's a beauty, right?

She just needs the right people. I turned away six couples who wanted to buy her. They weren't a good fit."

I snort at her approach to the real estate business, finally finding a smile that isn't laced with anxiety. "I think you've got that backwards. It's the house that has to be right for the person, not the person who has to be right for the house."

Aunt Em shakes her head. "That's not how I roll. I walked through this house. I know her. She wants this particular owner. I'm sure they'll be a good match."

I chuckle because I can't commit to a lunch order if the waiter so much as raises an eyebrow at me. Aunt Em rolls through her life with total conviction in her choices.

I want to be like that, instead of constantly apologizing for taking up space in the world.

As if she is my security blanket, I cling to my Aunt Em's arm when a third car joins ours in front of the house.

A married couple gets out of the minivan. The woman reveals a pregnant belly that is near to bursting.

The woman looks to be about my age, though, at twenty-five, I'm still not sure I will ever be grown enough to start a family. Watching other people in their mid-twenties make these adult sorts of decisions always perplexes me. I don't understand how they got there, and what it must feel like to have those lofty responsibilities.

I took care of a stray dog on my lunch breaks, but that is the most I can relate.

Which is to say, not at all.

The couple talks animatedly with my aunt, who, in her mid-fifties, never decided to have children or marry. Aunt Em regales them with the statistics of the house they have on their sheet of paper in their hands: three bedrooms, one and a half baths, new furnace, privacy fence, good school district, and two miles from the ocean.

Aunt Em unlocks the door using a funky lock box that has a combination, and ushers the couple inside.

I try to stay out of their way as I listen to their thoughtful "oo" and "ah". I am embarrassed to have shown up while my aunt is working, wearing stained jeans with my hair a fright. Though, Aunt Em doesn't seem put out in the least that I am not camera-ready.

They move through the living room into the kitchen while my aunt narrates the perks of the home, but I hang back when I hear a faint whine.

My heart thuds erratically when the whimper becomes more audible, letting me know there is an animal in the house. I meander toward the sound, moving past the knickknacks on the mantle. It looks as though the homeowner perhaps has an affinity for sailboat replicas, along with one odd foot-tall angel figurine with her arms outstretched around an empty space, giving a hug to no one.

The first thing my eyes go to when I step into the quaint dining room off the living room area is the most beautiful Pomeranian pup I have ever seen in my entire life.

The second thing I see is a puzzle half-done atop the table.

I love puzzles. I left behind quite a few thousand-piece boxes since they don't pack up easily for the long trip. My fingers itch to search for more edge pieces, but I hold myself back, since this is not my home.

The third thing I notice is a woman's leg sticking out from under the long tablecloth of the rectangular dining table.

My intake of breath is audible over the dog's soft cries. "Oh! Um, are you okay?" I ask the person as I move toward the table. I squat down and then tilt forward on my knees because it is physically impossible for me to be in the same room as a dog and not pet them.

I should be focused on the woman who fell asleep at random under her own dinner table, but the Pomeranian is too adorable for words. She is gorgeous, with reddish-blondish-brownish-colored hair that poofs like a little pom-pom. Her fluffy forward-curling tail wags while she whines, as if she is worried, but not as much anymore because I am here.

Maybe I am projecting, pretending the dog immediately loves me. My heart desperately longs to be adored by a furry bundle of cuteness.

My voice is soft with affection while my fingers run through her fur. "There, there, cutie pie. Let's see what happened. I'm sure your mommy is just fine. I..."

But my next words die on my tongue the moment I pull

back the blue tablecloth. The woman sprawled under the table is not, in fact, napping in an unusual spot.

The white-haired woman who looks to be in her late seventies is lying supine under the table. Her eyes are open, staring at the underside of the table. Her lips are rounded in a silent scream, frozen from the time this poor woman met her untimely end.

I wonder if her Pomeranian pup heard her final cry for help.

I fall back, scrambling away from the gruesome sight I did not expect to find on my first day in Apple Blossom Bay.

2

POMERANIAN WITNESS

I don't remember at what point my silent scream turned audible, but it doesn't stop until Aunt Em comes racing around the corner. She stops short, her hand flying over her mouth. "Hannah, what... Oh, Barb!"

My own horror leaps from my face to hers while the couple trails in behind my aunt with curiosity piqued. It's soon a jumble of shouts mingled with questions to which no one has the answers. It's only when I tug out my phone and call the emergency hotline that sense begins to return to my brain. Finally, I have a short list of ways to be helpful.

Call the cops.

Pet the dog.

I'm good with lists, so I stick to mine as if it is my job.

I speak in clipped sentences to the hotline operator, and finally get the story out as I understand it, including the address where the police can begin their investigation. I don't get off the floor, even when the police show up ten minutes later. Instead, I hold the dog on my lap, clinging to the comfort as much as the pup will let me. The two of us huddle in the corner of the dining room together.

I think we both need a solid hug.

There are three people in uniforms poking at the body and asking questions. Even though I don't know the first thing about conducting an investigation, my mind is latching onto errant things around the room so I can make a list of clues for myself.

Perhaps I have watched a few too many crime scene shows when I should have been looking for a job that paid more than minimum wage and didn't send me home stinking of gasoline.

There don't look to be signs of a struggle in this neat as a pin home.

The woman—"Barb," my aunt keeps repeating in a quavering voice—is clad in sweatpants and a t-shirt that reads "World's Best Grandma" in bright neon pink with a cutout of a baby's face printed into the material.

So, the woman has a grandchild. I can surmise that much.

The dog cuddles into me. I hold her closer while I run my fingers over her velvety ears. The poor dear. Sitting alone in this house with her deceased owner is no way to live.

My gaze trails over the dining room. I notice the tablecloth is there and the table has been set for two, with the puzzle pieces scattered in the center. Does that mean she lives with someone, or was she expecting company? Or perhaps the table was set for the showing.

"Aunt Em?" I ask in an unsteady voice. "Did the woman live here alone?"

It's then I realize my Aunt Emily is covering her mouth to hold in her shock and grief. She is standing in the archway that separates the dining area from the living room. "That's Barb Reeves. She lives here with her dog. I used to be in the Walking Bedhead Club with her. Sweet gal."

The married couple who were here to look at the house have excused themselves and gone home, no doubt wanting nothing to do with the house, now that it has hosted a dead body.

I add those tidbits from my aunt to my growing list of facts. I have no idea which details are important, so I commit them all to memory as best I can, mumbling them under my breath to the dog, who licks my chin to comfort us both.

I can't even fully enjoy the puppy snuggles because poor Barb Reeves is dead. The tablecloth has been lifted, so I can see Barb's body in sharper relief while the officers talk into their comms and discuss in hushed voices what should be done about the body.

I glance around the room for more clues to add to my little list while I kiss the top of the dog's furry head.

There doesn't seem to be any discoloration around Barb's mouth or bruising around her neck. In fact, if not for the obvious tells, I might think she simply fell asleep in an odd place and needed help getting up.

The police ask me a few questions, but when I prove completely unhelpful because all I know is what they can clearly see and surmise for themselves, I am allowed to excuse myself into the kitchen so they can talk to Aunt Emily. She knew Barb Reeves better than I did, being that I am a stranger here.

I glance around for the dog dish and then fish in the cupboards to fill it with the precious pup's dry food. I take note of the brand, which is for toy breeds, making me wonder just how old this dog is. I don't have an accurate frame of reference for predicting the age of canines, being that I've never owned one before.

Though not for lack of begging.

Every Christmas for years, I would plead with my parents to get me a dog. I pled for them to let me buy a dog myself and pay for the food and upkeep. But no matter how good my grades were, my parents were stalwartly opposed to having a pet of any kind in the house.

My fingers tingle with affection and warmth as I pet the dog while she eats with gusto. "I wonder how long it's been since you've had food in your tummy. Poor baby." My mouth pulls to the side. "Though, it can't be too many days because the body doesn't stink. Maybe the murder happened this morning or last night. If not for the foot sticking out from under the table, I wouldn't have known that your mommy was in the house at all." Compassion swells in me at the trauma this poor dog has gone through, having to see her owner like that.

I run my fingers over her ears. "You probably saw who did it, didn't you." I lean forward on my knees so I can kiss the top of her head.

My goodness, she's soft.

I run my hand along her collar until I find the nametag. I turn it so I can get a better look beneath the inches-long fur. "Cricket. That's a good name for an adorable dog. That's your name?"

At the sound of me saying her name aloud, Cricket's curled, bushy tail begins to wag.

I love this dog. I can't help it. Maybe it could be any old dog I came across in this dire situation, or perhaps it's because Cricket is absurdly lovable. Whatever the driving factor is, I don't stand a chance at resisting her precious face. Whatever she wants, I will make sure she gets.

I kiss Cricket again because I cannot help myself, and then I stand. "Let's get your things together. You are not staying here tonight." My voice is syrupy when I talk to her. She's been through so much. "Do you have any toys? I see you have a doggy door right there. Good job on not making a mess in the house, even though you've had such a stressful day."

I make a mental note that wherever Cricket lands, that house needs to have a doggy door. They also need to stroke her ears while she eats, because when I did that, she leaned into my touch.

She's a snuggler without a friend to hold, just like me.

Without thinking anything through or giving myself the chance to let logic stop me from caving to my childhood self, my legs carry me back into the dining room, where there is still a supine body in the middle of the scrum of officers.

I raise my hand, politely requesting an audience with the nearest man in uniform. "Officer?"

The older man with rust-colored hair turns to me, itching his mustache. "Deputy," he corrects me.

I dip my head. "Deputy, what happens to the dog?"

The man's eyebrow quirks at me. "Cricket?"

I nod, grateful this guy seems to know the victim well enough to understand this sweetheart dog should be cared for.

"Normally we reach out to the family to see if they can rehome the dog with them." He frowns. "But Barb's family lives out of state. I don't see that happening. They barely visited Barb. I can't imagine the dog would be at home away from the ocean, living with complete strangers. I don't know if they've ever even met Cricket."

My heart thumps unevenly in my chest. I am already so attached to this dog. I don't want her taken away from her home and her hometown in one fell swoop.

"What's the plan if they can't take her?"

The deputy scratches his reddish hair that is spiked in

the front and bare on his crown. "If that's the case, we would take any animals we find at a homicide to the shelter. Then they decide what's done with them."

My throat threatens to close.

I can't let that happen. If no one adopts her, then what? Is she put down? And during her time at the shelter, she'll be in a cage near a ton of other scared, barking dogs. She needs her ears rubbed on a regular basis.

I've always had a soft spot for animals that I haven't been able to suppress.

And I'm just vulnerable enough to voice it.

3

CRICKET'S NEW OWNER

My faded sneakers squeak on the floor as I shift my weight from one foot to the other. I keep my chin raised so I don't shrink away from finally speaking my truth and asking for what I want. "Would it be okay if *I* took Cricket home? Might be a better option than a shelter." I shake my head, realizing I haven't even given the officer my name, yet I'm hoping he trusts me with a dog. "I'm Hannah. Hannah Hart."

The deputy takes in my presence at the scene of the crime as if he is only just now noticing that I am a new fixture here. "Nice to meet you, Hannah Hart." He points to the nameplate on his uniform in lieu of verbally telling me his name. "You new in town?"

I motion to the living room area, where my aunt is talking to another officer. "I just moved here. I'm staying with my Aunt Em."

"Emily is your aunt?" Deputy Hanson quirks an eyebrow, remarking on our family affiliation with what sounds like approval. "Well, Hannah Hart, you got an ID?"

I nod so quick; I nearly lose my balance as I dart to the kitchen and grab up my purse. I produce my driver's license to the man, along with my phone number, which he jots down in a little notepad.

"It would be mighty helpful if you took the dog home today, maybe just for a few nights. We need to contact the family first, but at least that gives them a few days to decide what to do with the dog. They'll have to make a lot of decisions all at once when they get the news, so one less pressing thing would be a relief for a newly grieving family."

I bob on the balls of my feet with sheer glee. "Really? I can keep her for a few days?"

The corner of Deputy Hanson's mouth lifts, even though we are standing near a dead body. "I've never seen anyone so excited about dog sitting for no pay. Sure. I'll contact you once we hear what the family wants to do."

Joy overwhelms my body, flooding me with elation I have been waiting my whole life to feel.

I wasn't this happy when I graduated from high school or college.

I wasn't this excited when I bought my car with my own money from a job my parents said wouldn't do a thing for me.

But my euphoria comes crashing down when I realize I

haven't cleared it with the adult in the room, who should very much have a say in things. "Oh, wait. I need to discuss it with my aunt."

Deputy Hanson smirks at my words but aims his amusement away from me. "She won't put up a fight. Em's got a thing about taking in strays." He motions to himself as if he should be counted among the displaced who've been taken in by my vivacious aunt.

I turn with heavy shoulders to Aunt Em, who has just finished up with the other officer's questions. My fingers twist in the hem of my faded gray t-shirt. "Aunt Em, might it be okay if I…"

But before I can get out my entire request, Cricket yips at her, asking her for me when I start to clam up.

Aunt Em seems to understand. She bats her hand at us. "Do something good for yourself, Hannah Grapefruit. Plants are good for me, so I'm always messing with my flowerbeds in my backyard. You want to play with Cricket? I say go for it. Barb is a good woman. Of course we can take care of her dog." She grimaces. "Was." Then she shakes her head. "I don't want to think about it yet. But yes. Absolutely. Bring Cricket home with us. For a few days, for a few years. I'm a sucker for a good stray."

My heart swells to near bursting. Despite the dead body and the three officers milling about, I clear the gap between myself and my aunt and throw my arms around her, squeezing her tighter than I've hugged anyone in living memory.

Then again, I can't recall the last person I hugged. It had to have been several years ago because my body is unfamiliar with the practice. But I am so grateful that I take a chance and brave being bad at the very normal social exchange. I'm sure no one aside from me has ever overthought a hug this much, but I want to get it right.

My cheek presses to hers while I squeeze my aunt tight. "Thank you. I've always wanted a dog. This is my dream come true."

Aunt Em rubs my back through her chortle. She smells like roses freshly picked from the garden—a walking flower come to life. "Here's hoping all your wishes are fulfilled this easily."

When I pull away from our embrace, I realize my eyes are wet. I guess I wanted this chance more than I realized, because I rarely cry, at least not in front of people.

I whirl around and dart into the kitchen to pack up Cricket's things before this grand dream can be snatched away by pesky problems like life or logic.

"Would you like to come home with me, baby?" I ask in a voice so hopeful, it can only be described as emotional.

Cricket wags her tail at me, as if nothing could make her happier.

Joy overwhelms me as I place her bag of food on the counter, along with her now empty food dish and the water bowl. I find a bag of dog treats in one of the cupboards beside the leash, so those come with us, too.

I move around the house with renewed excitement

that pushes out the horror of the morning. I scour every surface for other things Cricket might need or appreciate.

A fluffy dog bed in Barb's bedroom on the floor beside her bed goes in my pile. Cricket will want to feel at home away from her home.

A chewed tennis ball that I assume is important in some way to Cricket goes on the counter, added to the things.

One item that catches my attention is that Barb's bed looks like it hasn't been slept in. The pink comforter with lace trim is perfectly in place, with pillows—both decorative and practical—taking up space like a floor model for the perfect bedding set.

Cricket comes in beside me, wagging her tail as she sniffs around my feet.

Instead of treating her like a dog, I pretend she is my very best friend with whom I share all my secrets. "The bed is made. So, either Barb died last night before she went to sleep, or she passed this morning, but not before she was properly awake enough to make her bed." I lean down and scratch the top of Cricket's head. "Judging by the lack of decay on the body, my guess is that she passed this morning. No signs of forced entry, either. Perhaps she knew her killer." My mouth pulls to the side. "Then again, she had that combination lock box on her front door for realtors to use when they show houses. It could be that someone broke into the box and used the key, which puts us back at square one in trying to figure out who hurt your mommy."

I want to know who would do such a thing to Cricket's owner. I feel a kinship the woman who doted on this precious pup. It makes me want to get to the bottom of who did this. Cricket deserves justice after such an upsetting upheaval.

I meander out into the dining room, where there is still a fair bit of investigative work going on, mostly centered around my aunt, it seems.

Aunt Em turns to me with a tired smile. "You ready to get going? I can follow you home. I had planned to show the Davidsons a few more houses, but for obvious reasons, they are done for the day."

I nod, but the deputy stops us. "Actually, we'll need you to come to the station, Emily." The man has a serious way about him. His chest is puffed to match his mildly pooched belly. He tucks his thumbs into the waist of his pants. His gait is wide as he draws himself up so he can claim the authority in the room, in case there was any question as to who is in charge.

He turns to me, his orange mustache twitching while he speaks. "New in town and you walk straight into a murder? Interesting timing you've got there, young lady."

Young lady? I've only been called that by my parents when I'm in trouble. Deputy Hanson looks to be in his fifties, so I don't question him, but I also don't like what he might be implying.

My hip juts to the side. "You're worried you've got a killer on your hands who murdered a woman in a house full of people, yet no one saw me do it?"

Deputy Hanson frowns at me. "Yeah, yeah." Then he motions to my aunt. "I still need you to come to the station, Emily. You had access to this house, so we've got to turn over all the stones we can to get to the truth of who did this to Barb."

My Aunt Em's spine straightens. "Do you think I'm the murderer?" She doesn't look indignant, but more annoyed that this is the route the deputy is taking. "I'm happy to answer any of your questions right here, Benjamin."

He shrinks at the use of his first name but holds his ground well enough to respond. "You have to know it's suspicious that you just so happened to come in here on the morning of the murder. You found the body with witnesses that could exonerate you if you were the killer, noting your shock over the body." He motions to me. "And a family member can hardly be counted as impartial."

Horror rises in my face, heating my cheeks. "What?" I croak.

My aunt rolls her eyes, nonplussed at the blatant accusation. "I'm so clever, aren't I? Clever enough to cheat myself out of the sale of this house."

Deputy Hanson seems finally able to read the room. He nods apologetically but doesn't backpedal even as his tone softens. "There was no sign of forced entry, and you just so happen to have the combination to the lock box where the key was stored, Emily. I have to do my job, and you have to let me."

Aunt Em's pink lips press together in dismay. "So, because I was near the body, I am the killer? That's some cracker jack detective work you're doing there. Glad I helped you study for your tests in middle school so many years ago. I can see we might have skipped a few key chapters on common sense."

They look to be of similar ages, though my aunt's way about her makes her seem far younger and more carefree, whereas Deputy Hanson's curmudgeon demeanor makes him come across as older.

It's amazing what a simple smile can do.

"I have to do my job, Em," the deputy reminds her.

Aunt Em nods stiffly. "I guess you're right. Best get my statement on the record so you can go out and look for the actual killer."

"That's the spirit." Deputy Hanson motions to the front door.

Aunt Em turns to me, and I can tell she is trying to iron the stress from her supermodel-like features. "Hannah, don't worry about a thing."

I shake my head, pleading with this man whom I don't know. I hope he will take me seriously. "Aunt Em can't possibly be a suspect. We were just in the wrong place at the wrong time. Or the right place, maybe. Barb Reeves could have been left here for who knows how long if my aunt hadn't come in here and discovered the body.

She should be thanked for her help, not presumed guilty."

Deputy Hanson tilts his head at my aunt. "Don't make this harder for me than it already is. Like I said, this is the quickest way to exonerate you."

Aunt Em shoots him a dubious look. "Is that what you said? Because I could have sworn you borderline accused me of murder. Amazing policework, by the way. When you don't have a proper suspect, go with the people who called in the murder."

Deputy Hanson turns to me. "Do you have proof of your whereabouts this morning, young lady? How did you end up here?"

Terror coats my insides, but logic wins out and pushes my hand into my purse. "I was driving into town, so I am nowhere close to being on your list of suspects." I fish around in my purse with unsteady fingers until I pull out a gas station receipt that proves I wasn't even in the state three hours ago. "Proof enough?"

The deputy takes a picture of the receipt with his cell phone and then tucks the device away. "Thank you. We have to do a thorough job. You understand."

I really don't, but I am not brave enough or disrespectful enough to mouth off to a police officer.

Deputy Benjamin Hanson seems to read my unspoken sass, because he adds, "Looking at everyone who could possibly have been the killer is my way of paying respect to Barb's memory, doing what I do. I can't bring her back, but

I can track down her killer." He lowers his chin. "I used to clean out her rain gutters in exchange for blueberry pie when I was a teenager. Barb was nice to me when I was a punk kid. I want to do this investigation right."

It's then that I see the sincerity in his brown eyes, and my attitude dies down considerably.

"I understand. But my aunt is innocent, so I'm going with her after I drop Cricket off at the house."

The deputy nods at me, as if he expected as much. Then he turns to my aunt. "After you, Emily. Let's get your statement at the station."

Aunt Em pulls herself up sanctimoniously, as if she has never deigned to be escorted anywhere by someone who questions her integrity. "Don't worry about a thing, Hannah, dear. I'll be home before you know it."

She moves out the front door with her nose in the air, carrying herself with dignity and daring mere minutes after being accused of murder.

4

TOURING THE TOWN

I want to do a proper job of introducing Cricket to her new temporary home, but I rush through the basics once I walk her from my clunky red sedan into Aunt Em's house. "Okay, Crick. You went to the bathroom outside at your house, so you should be good for the hour or so it takes me to hold Aunt Em's hand at the station." I shake my head as I set down the bag of dog food and assorted pet accoutrement in the front room. "I can't believe I have to say things like that. You know Aunt Em didn't do it. I mean, you would have growled or something when you saw her if she'd hurt your mommy."

Then again, the way Cricket gave me her unquestioning trust and got in the car with me the moment I offered my hand gives me pause. Not all dogs are guard dogs. Not all of them have a keen sense of which human did what.

I kneel beside her and run my fingers over the velvet of her dainty ears. "But you're a sweetheart, aren't you. I'm sure you couldn't fathom anyone being cruel because you're such a kind soul." I lean in, my heart swelling when Cricket cranes her neck toward me so she can lick the tip of my nose.

I swoon because I am a sucker for a doggy kiss. My arms go around her neck and, miracle of miracles, she lets me hold her when I don't have all the answers. Cricket loves me simply because I exist. I don't have to be impressive. I don't have to have chosen the right major or degree. I don't have to have an intimidating job with a flashy salary.

I love her. Thus, I am enough.

Emotion builds behind my eyes, but even though we are alone, I stuff it down so I can better serve my aunt when she needs me. Or, at least, when she needs someone with her to hold her hand.

Then again, my aunt is so self-possessed that I doubt this is shaking her up as much as it is me. I am the one who is more prone to worry.

I kiss Cricket's face before I release her. "I'll be back soon. When I come home, I'm going to give you all the snuggles you could possibly ever want. In exchange, I'm going to ask you not to tear up Aunt Em's furniture or break anything. Deal? We're new here; we don't want her to kick us out."

Cricket wags her tail at the attention, which I am going

to pretend is affirmation that she is on board with the rules.

I give her one more kiss because, obviously one is not enough. Then I stand, grabbing up my purse and heading out of the house.

My GPS informs me there is exactly one police station in Apple Blossom Bay, so I head that way. The city itself is small, taking up a total of six square miles, most of which are occupied by the beach. There are larger cities on either side, but this place still maintains its beachy small-town vibe. Each corner I turn looks like it should be on a postcard with "Wish You Were Here" printed across the top. The homes are brightly colored, including a hot pink one that makes me smile. I would never be that bold. Then again, I've only ever rented an apartment, so choosing a color for a house has never been an option for me.

Every lawn is well maintained. The flowerbeds all look like they are treated with love. The sunshine sparkles on the sidewalk as I drive slowly into town.

There is a little shop with a sign over it that reads "Sea Shell Smells" and another store that has been named "Bait, Tackle and Cuckoo Clocks".

My attention is diverted from the emergency at hand when I take in the quirky nature of the small town that seems a lot like my aunt—cheerful, odd, and perfect.

Why would a store sell bait, tackle, *and* cuckoo clocks? Those two categories have no connection in my mind.

Another shop called Apple Blossom Butter catches my eye.

What's inside that store? Random butters? Apple butter? Is there more than one kind of apple butter? I've never been much of an adventurous cook myself, so I don't know the ins and outs of the butter world.

But now I have to know.

Not *right* now, though. First things first: I need Aunt Em's name cleared of all suspicion.

So what if she had access to the key of the home where a dead body was found?

So what if Aunt Em skipped past the dining room, which was on the way to the kitchen when she was showing the house, leaving me to find the body, so she didn't have to discover it?

None of those things mean she is guilty.

She took me sledding when I was little. Obviously, people who create wild moments for sheltered girls aren't murderers.

Though, perhaps Deputy Hanson will require more proof than that.

It doesn't take me long to get to the station. I would imagine it doesn't take long to get anywhere in this city, even though the speed limit is a whopping twenty-five miles per hour throughout the entire place.

When I pull into the station, I take a deep breath, amping myself up to walk into a stressful situation.

Stress is not my jam, which I'm sure is true for everyone. But I make it a point to steer clear of confrontations and situations where I might have to rely on sticking with my decision when opposition surely comes.

I cave often, but not all the time, I remind myself. My parents warned me not to feed the stray dog who came around the gas station where I worked, begging for food. They said he would never leave me alone if I fed him.

Little did they know, I was hoping for exactly that.

Still, sticking to my gut and feeding that stray day after day was a bold step. Perhaps it was the last bold thing I did for myself.

I swallow my perpetual self-doubt and step out of the car, prepared to hold my aunt's hand while she taps into her well of bravery.

My faded sneakers are quiet on the sparkly, sunlit pavement. If I wasn't about to discuss a murder, it would be a lovely day.

The precinct is about what one might expect a small-town space to be. There is a tiny waiting area butted up to an empty reception desk, with a cavernous space behind it where the real action goes down.

I wait at the desk, unsure how to get where I need to be if no one is here to let me into the off-limits space.

I chew on my lower lip when I hear mumbling voices in the back. I decide to make my presence known by clearing my throat.

Still nothing.

Finally, I raise my voice as much as I am able without

violating my parents' "speak at a reasonable volume even when there's a fire in the house" unspoken rule. "Excuse me?"

Finally, a set of shoes shuffles my way, revealing the unwelcoming and unshaven face of Deputy Hanson. "Come on back, Hannah Hart."

I nod, feeling as if I'm violating some rule when I follow him behind the desk and move into the back area that is definitely for employees only.

And apparently, for murder suspects.

He keeps his voice quiet as he points to a stack of donuts. "I know it's cliché to have donuts at a police station, but those are seriously the best in the world."

My brows lift. "The world? Well, I don't believe it. Had you said the city, I would nod along. But the world?"

Deputy Hanson frowns at me, though not unkindly. "I'm fairly confident that you'll take one bite and agree."

I shake my head. "I'll try one after my aunt's name is cleared. A celebration donut."

Hanson nods. "Deal. In that case, we'll have to spring for fresh donuts. Those have been sitting there since yesterday."

I gawp at him. "You offered me a stale donut?"

The deputy shrugs, snatching one up as we pass the box. "They're fantastic no matter what day Dale fried them up."

My aunt does not look frightened or irritated that she is sitting in a hard plastic chair in the middle of the day when she could be out making a commission on the sale of a home to an eager young couple. "Hi, Hannah. Is your first day in Apple Blossom Bay as exciting as you had hoped?"

"Even more thrilling," I reply with a wry smile. "Maybe tomorrow we can go to the cuckoo clock shop and get accused of bird napping."

Aunt Em snorts, her shoulders rolled back as if this whole ordeal is nothing to be worried about.

I wish I could approach anything in life with that sort of confidence and polish.

I take the seat beside her while Deputy Hanson examines his notebook and poises his pen to the page. "You said you hadn't been to the house this week, but you'd contacted Barb last week to set up the showing."

My aunt nods. "That's right. She was going to be out of the house, so I could show prospects around."

"Because you're a realtor this month, right?"

She nods, and I can't decide if he's mocking her or not. He says it matter-of-factly, but the phrasing hits me the wrong way. As if there's something wrong with starting a new career in one's fifties.

My jaw tightens at the tone the deputy takes with my aunt.

Aunt Em leans back in her seat, her long billowy blue silk sleeves sliding down her forearms. "I like finding the right house for the right person. I looked at fourteen houses before I found this one for the Davidsons. It was perfect, but I doubt they'll be interested now, since the previous owner died in the house."

"How many houses have you shown them of those fourteen?"

"Just Barb's. It was a perfect match."

The deputy writes that down, as if it's some unfavorable clue.

I feel the need to jump in and defend my aunt, though she's said nothing scandalous. "She's a purist," I explain.

I might not be able to speak up for what I want all the time, but I can find my voice when my aunt is being made to look foolish with a simple twist of a question.

"My aunt didn't want to waste their time, so she scouted ahead to find the perfect home for the Davidsons. That's being thorough, not mischievous."

The deputy nods, his gaze connecting with mine as if to silently ask me why I think my input is necessary.

He turns back to my aunt. "Was Barb glad to be selling?"

Aunt Em's spine compresses a little, so she doesn't sit as straight in her seat. "Not particularly. She loves life in the Bay. But her children needed money, so she was going to sell her house to help them out, and then move in with them to look after her grandchild."

Deputy Hanson makes another note. "Anything else you want to tell me before we wrap up?"

Aunt Em leans forward and boops the man's nose, which turns his ears pink. "Yes. You are doing a great job,

Benjamin. Other than bringing me in as if I have anything to do with the murder, I think you're nailing it. Maybe next time, start with an actual suspect, rather than the family who called in the murder."

I press my lips together to fend off a giggle.

I can tell Benjamin Hanson does not care for being babied, but he is too turned around to brush aside her doting. "Yeah, yeah. I'll let you know if we find anything helpful in the case. But for the next week or so, don't leave town, alright?"

Aunt Em's mouth pulls to the side. "How about the edge of town? I have plans on the hill after the next rainstorm."

The deputy nods. "That's fine."

Aunt Em stands up, so I go with her, grateful I seem to have missed the worst of the interrogation.

I guess things in Apple Blossom Bay aren't altogether simple and sweet. It seems like there is a definite scandal lurking beneath the smiles this town has to offer.

If I want my aunt's name cleared, I'm going to need to get to the bottom of what happened to Barbara Reeves.

5

NEW DOG, NEW HOME

*W*hen we get home, I am relieved to find that Cricket did not chew up anything, and no messes are anywhere in sight. In fact, she seems happy to see me. Her feather duster tail wags with gratitude when I reach down to run my fingers over her fur. There is precious little I do not love about this dog, including the sweet way this baby greets me.

Aunt Em wastes no time showing me around the house. She has lost none of the pep in her step, even after being questioned at the police station. I feel bad for her and want to tell her she can show me around later, but she talks so much; I can't seem to get a word in.

"And here's the kitchen. Don't you love purple? Everything is purple in here, in all different shades. Purple is my creative color, and I love to be creative in the kitchen."

"Then that's a good place to have it," I motion around

to the walls, which are lavender. The cupboards are a deep eggplant, almost black. The floor is plum-and-gray checked. All her utensils and pots are bright purple. The whole thing is pleasantly overwhelming. It suits her bubbly personality well.

When the front door opens with no accompanying knock or doorbell, my spine stiffens. I grab up the pot on the stove because it is the nearest object that might prove useful to hurl at someone in an altercation. Cricket yips, though it's not loud enough to frighten away a burglar.

When Aunt Em laughs at my fright, I start to remember I'm not in in the big city anymore. "I'm in the kitchen!" she alerts the intruder.

When a friendly smile pops around the corner, I realize I am completely out of my element.

"Hey, Em. I brought over the posterboard and markers you needed to make the 'Welcome, Hannah' sign, but I can see I'm too late." The newcomer walks with a spritely pep about her. She lifts onto the balls of her feet like a curvy yet slender ballerina. She wears her long box braids in a sleek ponytail, making me wish I didn't look like I've been on the road for days the first time I meet my aunt's friend. "Is this her? Are you her?"

I set down the pot and extend my hand to the stranger. "I think so. I'm Hannah, Emily's niece."

The woman, who looks to be about my age, drops her posterboards and a case of markers onto the floor so she can ignore my outstretched hand and throw her arms around my shoulders. "It's amazing to meet you! I'm Jada. Jada Williams. Em's been talking about you for weeks. Do you like your room? I helped decorate it. Well, my kids and I."

I laugh at her exuberant nature. "That's nice. I haven't made it to the bedroom yet. We just started the grand tour. How many kids do you have?"

Jada grins at me proudly. "Twenty-two."

My eyes widen as I envision twenty-two children crammed into a house together.

Jada laughs at my befuddlement. "I'm a kindergarten teacher. I had the kids make paper flowers to welcome you to the town. They're on a vase in your new room."

I smile at the miscommunication. "Oh! That makes a lot more sense. You live nearby?"

"The school isn't far from here, so I stopped by after we got out for the day." She turns to my aunt, displaying the art supplies and posterboard. "This enough?"

Aunt Em nods. "Should be."

Another woman comes in from the front room, but this time I don't grab the pot to defend us against the intruder. It seems this is how life goes in Apple Blossom Bay. You leave your door unlocked, and people filter in and out when they feel like it.

I cannot imagine doing that in the city.

Cricket barks, but it sounds more like a friendly greeting than an alert we have to beware.

"Cricket? What are you doing here? Having a little adventure for the day?"

Em lights up. "Phyllis! Oh, good. I was hoping to give my little niece a proper welcome into town."

The woman with short gray curled hair comes into the kitchen, showing off a lavish ballgown that sticks out as strange in the middle of this spring weekday. "Oh, fiddle-sticks!" The woman in her seventies says when she sees me. "I was hoping to get here before you did. Oh, well." Phyllis reaches into her purse and pulls out a fistful of confetti, which she blows in my face. "Welcome to Apple Blossom Bay!"

I sneeze and then cough as the metallic glitter goes partially up my nose and into my hair.

Jada groans. "I'm telling you, Phyllis, you have to find a different thing to blow at people. How about flower petals? Those are pretty and they don't get stuck in people's hair and clothes for a fortnight. Glitter is my arch enemy." She holds up her hands. "Hazards of being a kindergarten teacher."

I smile as the glitter cascades off my skin and clothes. "It's nice to meet you, Phyllis." I motion to her peach gown. "You look nice. Are you going somewhere special?"

"No," Phyllis answers lightly. She straightens a ruffle as she hums to herself. "Just seemed like a nice day to do something good for myself."

Her words chime in my ear, sounding like the exact ones Em said to me when I asked her if I could take

Cricket home. I love the sentiment but can't remember the last time (other than asking for the dog) that I purposefully did something good for myself.

I'm not sure I would know where to start with that one.

Jada brushes some of the glitter off my shoulders, giggling softly. "Phyllis is our best dressed resident of Apple Blossom Bay. Em, Phyllis, and Dorothy are always trying to drill into my head that it's important to do something good for yourself, and they lead by example."

I take in the purple kitchen with new eyes. This whole place is an explosion of my aunt's quirky personality. I can't help but fall in love with it because it is uniquely her. If she hadn't done something good for herself and followed her purple bliss, then she would have a perfectly fine, ordinary kitchen.

I love that Phyllis and my aunt seek out ways to do something good for themselves.

Aunt Em motions for Phyllis to come in and take a seat at the round table in the kitchen. "Did you do it? Did you handle the business cards?"

"Business cards?" I inquire. I feel even more out of place now in my stained jeans and t-shirt in comparison with Phyllis' lovely gown. I wish I'd had time to indulge in a shower before meeting my aunt's friends.

Phyllis' gray hair is pinned in small ringlets away from her round face. When she sits at the table in the corner of the kitchen, she nods. Then she reaches into her flower-bedecked purse and smacks a business card atop the table.

"I think this will do it. I set out a stack of your business cards at the hardware store, and Larry took a pile to the Forgotten Stock Market. That's the last place on my usual route. Kept this one for myself, so I can refer you on the go."

Aunt Em nods her approval. "That's perfect. Thank you."

I love how supportive Em's friend is.

Jada claps for Phyllis' extra legwork. "Well done." She leans down and pets Cricket, who laps up the attention. "Are you dog sitting for Barb?" she asks Aunt Em.

My aunt's smile falls. "Sort of. You might want to sit down, Jada." She motions to another chair at the table. "It's been an eventful morning. I was showing Barb's house today to a couple it would have been perfect for, but when we got inside, Barb was..." She pauses, swallowing hard. "Barb was dead."

I grimace at the frank explanation.

The questions one might expect come hurtling out at us. "What?" "How?" "Who could have..." and more hit the air with a sadness that even Cricket feels.

The poor baby whines and nudges her head into my leg, so we can be sad together.

I'm not sure if you're supposed to pick up Pomeranians (she has such short legs but also looks decently solid), but I find I can't help myself. The urge to pick her up and rock her like a baby is strong.

I lean down and lift the solid little fluffy lump while

Aunt Em tells the girls about our morning. Though I've never done this before—with a dog or a baby—I manage to pick her up in a tender hold where her hindquarters rest on my hip and her front paws drape around my neck. She stabilizes herself on my hip to compensate for my missing right hand, rather than wiggling around and risking a fall.

The two of us sigh in perfect unison. Her dog breath fans across my face like a sweet breeze when I have gone my whole life suffocating.

This is it. This is the hug I have needed. The rocky and jagged parts of my soul begin to smooth over the longer Cricket lets me hold her like this—the furry baby on my hip.

While I wouldn't normally feel comfortable chatting with people I don't know, with Cricket on my hip, my tongue unties itself when Em is peppered with more questions than she can field by herself. "We don't know how or who. Barb was underneath her dining room table, her body hidden by the tablecloth. I'm guessing she didn't do that to herself. The police are doing their thing, but it's looking like foul play."

Jada gasps while Phyllis lets out a mourning cry that tugs at my heart.

Whatever day these ladies were expecting to have, the sunshine of the morning is gone, replaced by a dark cloud hovering in the kitchen.

6

DO SOMETHING GOOD FOR YOURSELF

I don't know what to do in these sorts of situations, so I cast around my aunt's purple kitchen to see what kinds of things she likes that she might want to comfort her on this tumultuous day.

When my eyes fall on the tea kettle, my feet move toward the stove. Though I'm not all that well-versed in preparing anything other than gas station coffee, I'm guessing tea is the thing people want to be holding or stirring when they hear horrible news. I am new to this kitchen, and hopefully not overstepping too much as I pick up the kettle, making sure Cricket stays still on my right hip. I fill the kettle with hot water while the three talk about the friend they did not expect would meet an untimely end this very day.

After I turn on the burner, I fish in the cupboards for tea bags, grateful when I find a stash on the third attempt.

"Absolutely terrible," Jada remarks, her hand over her heart. "I was just at Barb's house two weeks ago, delivering a meat pie."

Phyllis and Aunt Em share a grimace. "Two weeks ago?" Phyllis questions. "That's good. We can rule out food poisoning, then."

Jada harrumphs at the two older women, who share a chortle. "I happened to have bought the meat pie on Hank's recommendation and dropped it off for her. It's not like I served Barb my beet casserole."

Aunt Em grimaces at the memory of Jada's failed beet casserole.

Though, what a successful beet casserole might taste like, I cannot begin to guess.

My aunt shakes her head. "Jada, you need to start with something simpler. Something that is bound to turn out. How about I show you how to make mashed potatoes again?"

Jada frowns. "Those mashed potatoes would have been good if I hadn't accidentally used vanilla soy milk instead of unflavored."

My expression twists at the thought of vanilla mashed potatoes.

Aunt Em turns to me—the person who is content to cuddle the dog in the corner and stay out of everyone's way. "Feel like joining us, Hannah Grapefruit?"

I gnaw on my lower lip, worried that I'm overstepping and taking up special bonding time between Jada and my aunt. My voice comes out a quiet squeak. "I wouldn't mind a cooking lesson, Aunt Em. My mashed potatoes aren't anything to write home about."

As if Cricket knows how hard it is for me to ask for help in any form, even guidance, she licks my cheek to applaud me for being brave.

Jada nods, her spirits lifting that she might not be the weakest link in the kitchen. We can be at the bottom rung together. "Yes! Let's do that. I still have those potatoes from the last time you taught me."

My aunt's expression sours. "Two months ago? Honey, throw those potatoes away. We'll start fresh tomorrow night. We'll make so many mashed potatoes, no one is going to want to look at another potato for the next year."

"Sounds good."

I pull down three purple mugs with peppy lavender dots on them. I'm grateful Cricket seems to understand that if she wants me to carry her on my hip, she can't wiggle around.

I notice one of us is not enthusiastic about massive quantities of mashed potatoes. "Phyllis, can I get you some tissues?" Though, she doesn't look like she is crying. Her brows are pushed together, and a frown is firmly fixed on her wrinkled face.

"No, dear. Got a lot on my mind, I guess. I never thought anyone would even raise their voice to Barb, much less do anything deadly. Though, now that I think about it..."

I pause while Jada and Aunt Em talk in detail about mashed potatoes. I migrate to Phyllis' side. "What's got you worried?" I ask.

Phyllis shakes her head as if she doesn't want to talk about it, but at my prodding, she opens up. Her eyes stay on her hands while she speaks. "It can't be relevant. I'm sure it's not. But the timing is..." She turns to me, garnering Aunt Em and Jada's attention. "I went to deliver roses from my garden to Barb last week. I usually just walk right on in, but I heard yelling, so I stayed on the porch until the shouting calmed down."

I sit in the chair beside Phyllis that Jada abandoned, shifting Cricket from my hip to my lap. "Who was Barb yelling at?" I press, leaning in because I need this information. I don't want police officers sniffing around my aunt, thinking she is a suspect.

My fingers trill over Cricket's reddish-brownish-golden fur. I love the way she cuddles into me, as if knowing that I need a hand to hold if I am going to be this interactive with new people.

Phyllis chortles at my question. "Oh, Barb wouldn't yell at a soul. No, it was some man yelling at her. I didn't get a name. I didn't ask. When he left, I saw him in passing." She raises her hand to indicate his height. "A little taller than me but not much. Brown suit and matching shoes, wearing a bowler hat, which I thought strange, because it was real hot that day. I can't imagine someone wanting to wear a suit for the fashion when it was so warm out." She shrugs. "But then again, it's important to do something good for yourself, right? Maybe bowler hats and suits are that man's version of bliss."

I mull over that reoccurring sage sliver of advice.

Do something good for yourself isn't an altogether foreign concept, but usually when I finally gather the courage to ask for something I want out of life, I am reminded that stepping too far out of bounds and reaching higher than one's expected range is generally frowned upon.

Then again, I am sitting at a table with a woman in a lovely gown, holding a dog that is most certainly not mine.

Maybe I can learn a thing or two from these women.

Phyllis touches her mug of tea but doesn't pick it up. "I'm not sure how anyone could yell at Barb like that."

I take a chance and reach out to hold Phyllis' hand when her sadness spikes. "Did Barb mention anything about him?"

Phyllis shakes her head. "Not a thing. I asked her who he was, and she brushed off my question. Said he was of no concern, and thank you for the flowers and all that." She lowers her chin. "I should have pressed harder. I should have stayed until the story came out."

"How could you have known it would go south like this?" Jada offers, and I nod along.

I take out my phone and call the number on the business card the police officer gave me. "I'm thinking the deputy would like to hear this. Give him someone to chase after instead of the woman who happened to be at the wrong place at the wrong time."

Phyllis and Jada whip their heads at Aunt Em. "Deputy Hanson doesn't suspect you, does he?" Jada asks, scandalized. "He couldn't possibly."

Aunt Em brushes off the fact that she is the only person on the list of suspects as if it's all no big deal.

I grip my phone as I resolve myself to get the attention off my aunt and onto whomever it is who yelled at Barb that day.

7

OCEAN FISH MARKET

*B*eing new in town has me feeling like a fish out of water, especially when I go to the fish market, and everyone has their own rhythm to things that I simply don't fit into. I duck when a fish is thrown inches from my face, from one seller to another.

A glitter shower was one thing, but if I come home with fish residue in my hair, I will have something to say about it.

"You should probably duck when that happens again," Jada chuckles at my wide eyes after taking a sip of her to-go cup of coffee. "This is the Ocean Market Strip." Jada spreads her free arm out proudly. "Everything fresh, right at your fingertips."

"I feel like you drew the short end of the stick, babysitting me today," I tell her, looking around wildly to make sure I don't walk into an errant flying fish. "When I told

Aunt Em that I was going to explore the town, I didn't mean for her to make you cancel your plans."

Jada bats away my concern. "Are you kidding me? I'm not cancelling anything. You're going to help me learn how to make mashed potatoes, which was my big plan. And you're helping me run errands while I show you the town. It's a perfect fit."

Jada is easy to like. She has a bubbly personality and treats me as if I am not an inconvenience.

She doesn't even mind that I brought along Cricket for the tour.

"Well, I appreciate it. After finding Barb yesterday, I'm not ready to go to another house for sale with my aunt."

As if to agree with me, Cricket barks twice.

I feel you, sister.

I've got Cricket on her leash, and I am loving every minute of it. I've always wanted to walk a dog. The stray who visited me behind the gas station didn't come with a leash, of course. The market in town is high stakes territory for this being my first time walking a dog. There are so many different smells and sounds in a fish market. If I am overwhelmed, I know Cricket has to be on hyperdrive, too.

Though, I'm guessing this scene is quite normal to Cricket, since this is her hometown. Whereas I am struggling to take it all in, she wags her tail happily.

The ocean breeze keeps the tang of the fish stink from becoming stifling or sticking inside my nose for too long. The cacophony of chipper shouting as a fish is thrown from one person to another before it is wrapped in newspaper and handed to a patron is a lot to take in. I'm afraid if I blink, I will miss something, or I'll be bludgeoned in the side of the head with a dead fish.

Jada points to a table that has fresh vegetables on one side and live lobsters in a tank on the other. "That's Randy. He says he sells the best lobsters on the strip, but honestly, it's almost not worth it. He talks your ear off so much that it's faster to jump into the water and fish one out yourself. Sweet guy, but don't stop to browse at his booth unless you have an hour to spare."

I chuckle at the couple being held captive by conversation while the man with swarthy forearms gesticulates wildly. "Okay, Randy is either telling them he can swim like a dolphin, or he's saying that he is a human tornado."

Jada snorts. "I really hope it's the latter. I'd very much like to see that." She points to a woman in her fifties standing behind a fish jerky booth. "That's Melinda. She sells all sorts of jerky that she makes herself. Her son is Pete, who graduated from high school last year. He's a lifer, like me."

"A lifer?" I inquire.

"You know. Someone who's born here and never leaves."

"You were born here and never moved out? That's nice. It's a beautiful place to live." I breathe in the sea air, wondering if the varying sights and smells might dim over time, their novelty fading. As it is now, I am enraptured at the lively market. It seems to sell mainly things centered around the catch of the day, but with the occasional oddity thrown in to give the place variety.

Jada shrugs while we strut around like two women who have the cutest dog in the entire world and not a care on our shoulders. "I like it here. There's always something going on. Something to look forward to. Something to get dressed up for. Plenty of lifers with a mix of visitors who are just in for the week to see the sights."

I recall the peach frilly dress Phyllis wore yesterday. "I liked Phyllis' dress. Is there anything coming up I should be looking forward to? I mean, now that I live here, I should do some town things."

Jada hooks her arm through mine as if we've never had secrets between us. I've never had anyone take to my wallflower ways as easily as she does. Jada has that way about her that instantly makes you feel like you belong.

Oh, how I want to belong.

Jada grins at me. "You're going to do exactly that today. Town things. We're going to skip rocks down at the pier."

"Skipping rocks? That's..." I mean, I don't know what to say about a non-event like that. "I don't remember the last time I've skipped a rock. I'm not sure I've ever tried."

Jada grins at me as if she's just suggested going to a theme park and convinced me to go along for the wild ride.

Hey, I'm not one to judge. If this is what counts as a fun time in Apple Blossom Bay, then I'm all in. Not like I was killing it with adventure in the big city. There were theaters, clubs, restaurants, and museums, but I never had the courage to go out on my own and see much of it.

Maybe I just needed Jada to drag me along on her adventures for me to find a few of my own to enjoy.

Jada stops at Melinda's booth. "Hey, Melinda. This is Em's niece, Hannah. She's new in town, and if she's never skipped rocks before, then I'm guessing she's never tried fish jerky before."

I smile to keep myself from blanching. I am not hugely adventurous in my dining experiences. If fettuccini alfredo is on the menu, that's what I'm ordering. Fish jerky?

I'm not a fan of beef jerky, so I cannot imagine this fishy version will be my new culinary obsession.

Still, I give Melinda a polite smile, knowing I can't clutch tightly my aversion to seafood and still call myself a resident of Apple Blossom Bay. I loop Cricket's leash halfway up my right arm and squeeze my forearm to my bicep to hold the strap in place. Then I reach out with my left hand to take the sample.

It feels leathery between my fingers and doesn't smell necessarily of fish. Though, everything smells like the ocean in this market, so I'm not sure I could pick out one note from another with any certainty.

I'm grateful when Jada starts a conversation with Melinda, so I can take my time psyching myself up to try a bite. "Shame some of the booths are closed. I was hoping to give Hannah Hart here the full experience."

Melinda's head bobs as she pulls out another piece of fish jerky, this time to give to Cricket. I'm guessing dogs don't hold the same reservations about jerky as I do. "Yeah. A few people are over at Barb's house today, boxing up her things for her daughter." She motions to the booth beside hers, which has a selection of shrimp on display, but no one manning the booth. "I'm pulling double duty for Shane while he helps out. Apparently, Barb's daughter wants her things packed up pronto so she can move on selling the place. She was a little rude about the whole thing on the phone, actually."

Jada leans her hip on the post at the edge of Melinda's booth. "Really? Doesn't her daughter live in New York? Does she want all Barb's stuff shipped to her, or is it being stored here until she can get to it?"

Melinda shrugs. "No idea. I stayed out of it." She harrumphs. "You'd think Barb's daughter would want to fly over here and take care of things, but apparently she can just yell, and Barb's neighbors will handle it all." Melinda straightens her glass containers of the jerky with a sharpness to her movements.

I can tell she's worked up, so I try my hand at empathy. "That sounds like a lot for you all to take on, especially on top of grieving the loss of a friend."

Melinda makes a noncommittal noise. "Sure. My son is all broken up about it, but honestly, I don't know why." She leans in conspiratorially. "You know I'm not about to say anything bad about a soul, but Barb is on my list. My son did her gutters for her just last week, and she didn't pay Pete a nickel. Not a nickel!" She leans back with her arms crossed. "Everyone's all bent out of shape about losing her, and I feel for them. I don't wish ill on nobody, but oh, it chaps me that Barb got away with not paying Pete. My boy is too sweet to call her out on it, and now it's too late."

I chomp down on the chunk of fish jerky just to keep myself from saying something salty. Whenever someone says they don't like to gossip and then indulges in a steaming heap of the stuff, it rubs me the wrong way. And being sore because a woman stiffed her son on a job? Sure, it stinks, but when a woman is dead, that's hardly the thing to be concerned about.

Jada selects a single piece of pineapple trout jerky, the sound of which makes me gag. She pays for her "treat," if that's what it is, and we go on our merry way, this time with less pep in our step.

I keep my voice down as we stroll through the Ocean Fish Market. "I feel dirty when someone speaks ill of a deceased person. I thought the consensus was that Barb was a sweet old woman. Now she's a woman who goes back on paying a teenager after he cleans her gutters? I don't need that swimming around in my head. I'm still trying to push out the image of Barb lying under that table when I found her."

Jada tilts her head sympathetically. "That's just Melinda. She's always sore about something. It's bad if you want to have a good day, but good if you're having a bad day and you need some fuel for the dumpster fire. No matter who it is in this town, she's got something to say about them. I'm sure when I kick the bucket, people will be sad, but Melinda will remember when I held a kid back instead of promoting them to the first grade. That was an unpopular decision." She takes a bite of her fruity fish jerky. "But see, I learned the secret to that."

I lean in with intrigue, a smile playing on my lips. "Oo. Tell me, tell me. What is it that makes you impervious to gossip?"

Jada holds out her hands to reveal her mantra. "I don't care."

I snort out a laugh at the unexpected succinctness to her philosophy. "Is that so?"

Jada shrugs. "I've never been the popular girl, so those sorts of social pressures mean precious little to me." She unbuttons her cardigan to reveal her t-shirt, which has multicolored handprints all over it. "See? If I cared about being popular, I'm not sure this is the fashion choice I would make." She hugs herself with a smile. "But I love my kids, and I loved little Jeremy enough to hold him back when he wasn't ready to go on to the next grade."

I have a new appreciation for Jada. "You know, I like that."

"I'm glad. You'll need that little life lesson in your back pocket from time to time."

Now that we're far enough away from Melinda's booth,

I feed the rest of my sample piece of jerky to Cricket, who devours the gift with more gratitude than I can muster.

We stop at a few more booths, and I start to realize that Cricket is leading the way, knowing which vendors give out free treats to dogs.

Little scamp.

My mind drifts while Jada greets the people she knows. I hang in the background, caring too much that I'll make a fool of myself and say the wrong thing.

I need to be more like Jada, who doesn't care about the things that are not important.

My mind drifts to poor Barb as I factor in the new seeds of information. Would this Pete kid be so put out about not being paid for doing Barb's gutters that he might strike out at her? Would he be angry enough over being stiffed to kill an old woman?

I don't know much about Barb or this town, but it seems like there is more to Apple Blossom Bay than I originally thought. I didn't realize that when I packed up my things, I was moving myself to a small town that is rife with drama.

8

BREAKING AND ENTERING

*W*hen we finish up with the fish market, Jada strolls by my side down the sloped walkway to the pier below. There are several boats tied to the dock with a few dozen people roaming about. They talk with each other animatedly; I'm guessing about how awesome boat life is.

I can't imagine what it must be like to have such a fantastic ocean view at your disposal day after day. Does it make the people here unwind that much more easily, or do they take it for granted?

I cannot imagine growing tired of the waves lapping at the shore, or the seagulls singing their own special tune. Cricket happily yips at the birds while we walk. My worn sneakers squeak on the wooden dock.

There is a big, black shiny boat with an awning over the back end docked partway down the row. It looks polished and new beside the other, less impressive boats. There's another with the name "Erma's Heart" painted across the side, and dozens more waiting to be taken out on the open waters.

Jada directs us toward a quaint boat that has what looks like a log cabin with a flat roof atop it, and a ladder leading up to the top. She points, but I am already in love. "Oh, wow! I've never seen a houseboat before in real life. That's what it's called, right?"

Jada nods. "What do you think?"

"It's so cool!" The urge to jump from the dock onto the houseboat taps me on the shoulder, but as I am a grownup who does not want to be arrested for trespassing, I hold myself back. "What a cool life that must be. To live on the lake? To be rocked to sleep by the water? Talk about living off the land. And to park your houseboat in Apple Blossom Bay is smart. Such a pretty town."

Jada chuckles at my enthusiasm. "If you've never seen a houseboat before, I'm guessing you've never been on one, either. Feel like going exploring?"

I gape at her, my volume shushing to the level of one conveying a scandal. "I can't do that! That's trespassing. Deputy Hanson and I didn't get off on the best foot, being that the first time he met me, I was next to a dead body. I'm guessing he won't be thrilled if the second time we meet, I am being hauled in for breaking and entering."

Jada's eyebrows dance with mischief. "Let's be daring.

I've got bail money." She jerks her chin toward the house-boat and steps down onto the thing without hesitation.

My hand goes over my mouth as my head darts this way and that. I hope no one sees us and calls the police. Jada's smile is wide as she waves me to come aboard.

I whisper-shout at her while Cricket barks twice, as if the sweet dog doesn't understand why I'm being a stick in the mud when there is adventure to be had.

Jada holds out her arms for my dog. Even though she's got tiny toy Pomeranian legs, Cricket trots off the ledge of the dock into Jada's arms, trusting that she will be caught and cared for.

What a precious pup. I had to take a similar leap, moving across the country, and trusting that Aunt Em and I would mesh. I had to trust a whole lot of things, actually. I had to trust that she wouldn't be another version of my parents, who would shame me into silence because I have basically done nothing meaningful with my life. They pointed me in the direction of their choosing, and when it didn't pan out their way, I was the failure.

Business degree. What was I thinking, going along with that? I don't have the gumption to run a business, much less an idea for one. I should have been stronger. I should have told my parents that a business degree wasn't the right call for me.

Jada waves for me to use the steps that she's tethered to the dock. "Come on! Life is for the living, and boats are for the stealing. Are you a mouse or a pirate?"

I chuckle at her phrasing. "Well, when you put it like that." I spread my arms out to the side uncertainly. "I guess I'm a pirate?"

Jada pumps her fist into the air. "That's the spirit!"

I glance around for signs of the authorities, waiting for me to step a toe out of line so they can haul me in for trespassing. But no one seems to notice or care that I am clearly breaking the law, taking my first step into life as a pirate.

Cricket barks to spur me on. Even though we have only known each other one whole day, Cricket just plain gets me. She watches my hesitation as my conscience and my "stay in line" nature battles with a need for adventure I didn't realize I had. Maybe it's been there all along, but I've done all I can to silence that cry for something more.

Staying inside the lines hasn't gotten me very far in life.

Perhaps I am destined for the path of a pirate.

Though my stomach is in knots, I do the impossible and take a leap toward the unknown. I hold my breath as I walk down the steps onto the platform of the houseboat. The rush of disobedience thrills me so much that goosebumps erupt down my arms. My spine straightens with purpose.

Jada claps to commemorate my daring. "Look at you, being all wild. Was it as scary as you thought, taking up the life of a pirate?"

I raise my nose. "Yes! Are you kidding me? I don't do stuff like this!"

Jada motions for me to follow her further into a life of crime. She shoots me a sneaky grin. "Come on. The good stuff is always in the house."

"The good stuff? What exactly are we hoping to find?"

"We're pirates, so we're looking for buried treasure and booze."

"So, a few bucks and wine coolers?"

"That's how I roll." Jada pops open the door, escorting Cricket and myself inside.

"Oh, it's cute! Look at that over there." I point to what looks like a very normal living room, including a couch with a television mounted to the wall. "The couch is pink and has white daisies on it. I love it!"

Jada grins at me as she moves to the refrigerator with ease. She takes out a juice box and hands it to me. "I'm glad you like it. I sewed the daisies on myself. Gotta do something good for yourself every now and then, right?"

My shoulders deflate after I lose a portion of my tension. "We're not breaking and entering. This is *your* houseboat!"

Cricket barks twice to let me know that I finally guessed it.

Jada snickers at my slow revelation. "I had you going there for a while. I'm impressed I was able to keep the secret this long. I'm still proud of you, though. You really thought we were breaking and entering." She lifts her chin. "You're still a pirate to me."

I press my hand over my heart at the sincere compliment I very much needed to hear. "Thank you. And now that I'm not worried about being arrested, I can actually enjoy my first time being on a houseboat." I look around, taking in what looks like a studio apartment set inside a furnished log cabin. "This is nice, Jada. I mean, hands down the coolest house I've ever visited."

Jada beams with pride. "Thanks. My parents weren't exactly thrilled when the house I was saving up for turned out to be on the water. But I'm happy here. I think I was part fish in my last life. If I'm away from the water for too long, I get antsy."

"Huh. I guess I never realized how deep that feeling might go in a person." I sit with her on the daisy-bedecked couch, sipping my juice box like a true child. "So, you're a kindergarten teacher. You live in the coolest house in the world. You have a fridge full of juice boxes. Tell me more."

Jada snickers while we sip our apple juice. "I'm a terrible cook, so don't be too impressed. Em, Dorothy, Edna, and Phyllis have taken me under their wings on more than one occasion to make sure I don't live off pretzels and apple slices. I'm sort of a lost cause in the kitchen, but I am amazing with scissors and paints." She settles into the couch, hitching her knee up between us so she can turn to face me more fully. "So that's me. Now it's your turn. Em's been gushing about her favorite niece who's coming to live with her, but that's all I know."

I smirk. "I'm her only niece, so I'm glad to hear I'm her favorite."

Jada moves her hand in a circular motion to get me to talk about myself. "Out with it, city girl."

I gnaw on my lower lip while Cricket takes her sweet time sniffing around the houseboat. "I guess there's not much to know. Grew up in Chicago. Graduated a couple years ago with a business degree, but I haven't found anything that sounds..." I trail off with another shrug. "Haven't found where I belong, I guess."

Jada motions around us. "Haven't found your houseboat?"

I smile at my new friend. I'm grateful she wants to invest the time it takes to force me out of my shell—a task I gave up on long ago. "I suppose that's exactly the sort of bliss I've been looking for. I thought that if I followed the path my parents laid out for me, I would land somewhere solid. But after graduation, all I've been able to feel is a void, like I'm in the wrong place with the wrong set of skills. I took a job I don't care about and didn't fight for a raise when I needed one. Rent went up and my income stayed at the same lackluster level it's always been. I have a business degree, but no interest in using it. My parents suggested I come here to be with Aunt Em, but I think their aim is for a change of scenery to somehow fix what's wrong with me." I say it like it's a joke, but the words taste like bitter sand on my tongue.

Jada tilts her head at me. "And what exactly do you think is wrong with you?"

I have no answer to that, only the directionless blah

I've never been able to shake. "I think that's what I came here to figure out."

Jada whistles to Cricket, who stops sniffing the corners of the house and turns toward the sound. She jumps up between us, wagging her fluffy tail happily, as if she can't believe her good luck that she is being included in girl time. "Well, for what it's worth," Jada says while she pets Cricket, "I'm glad you landed here. We'll find the thing that makes you come alive. If it's not where you've been, then I'll help you find it here."

My smile tugs to the side as I lean into the cushion. "You got a thing for lost causes?"

She doesn't laugh at my sort-of-a-joke-sort-of-serious-comment. Instead, she examines my fading smile. "Emily and I won't leave you hanging with no passion or purpose." She reaches out and rests her hand atop mine. "It's going to be okay, Hannah."

I blink at our hands, admiring the differing hues of our skin tones. I don't know why emotion rises so violently; I nearly choke. Nothing has felt "okay" in a very long time, if ever.

But at Jada's firm promise, the tension that's been building in my body since birth deflates in a gust.

Maybe I don't know everything about how to live life to the fullest, but one thing is sure: I'm glad I landed here.

9

THE FORGOTTEN STOCK MARKET

*A*fter our heart-to-heart, Jada insists we see more of the small town. I match my pace to her slower one, noting that everyone here seems to meander rather than beeline with purpose. More than a few times, I have to slow myself down, breathing in the ocean air to remind myself that I am in no hurry.

I haven't been to the grocery store in town, of which I have been informed there is only one. "Seriously? I can't fathom one store having everything Apple Blossom Bay needs."

Jada points to the store, which was a five-minute walk from her houseboat. "That's because you haven't been to the Forgotten Stock Market. Larry owns the store, and he keeps everything in perfect order. Larry's a burned-out stockbroker who moved here and opened up a grocery store." She nods to the building. "This is Larry's version of happiness. It's his houseboat, if you will." She smirks at me, driving our metaphor home. "If they don't have it, you don't need it." She motions to the lettering under the giant sign with a trout leaping out of the water, which reads exactly that as their slogan.

The building is larger than a corner store but smaller than a superstore. The red brick exterior is hemmed in by a sparkling sidewalk that I swear catches the sun at just the right angle to make the whole place appear as if nature is dancing around it. There are several tall apple trees dotting the parking lot. I spot red pots as tall as me with rose bushes popping out of the top.

I cast around as we approach, unsure what to do with a dog when one goes shopping. "Is there a bike rack I should tie Cricket to while we go in and shop?"

Jada bats away my concern. "No way. Cricket would miss out. She wouldn't forgive you for leaving her out here all by her lonesome. She lost her momma yesterday."

"But they won't allow dogs in there, I'm sure. We'll wait out here for you, then."

Jada takes the leash from me and strolls toward the front doors. "This isn't city life, Hannah. Time to breathe in that sweet Apple Blossom Bay breeze. This is your new home, babe. Best start taking up some space here."

I don't know how to do that. I mean, the whole of what I was taught growing up is to *not* take up space in the world, to apologize for the space you do take up, and plan to make zero waves in the future, so as not to make anyone uncomfortable.

But part of me craves the confidence Jada possesses, the ease with which she strolls into a store.

Tentatively, I follow behind Jada, expecting someone to shout at us to leave with our dog the second we enter.

But I am pleasantly surprised when a warm greeting comes our way. "Oh, Cricket! You poor baby." A store employee with a nametag reading "Betty" on her red vest waves us down and tugs a dog biscuit from a metal bowl near her register. "I've been saving your favorite treat right here." Then she calls over her shoulder. "Everyone, Cricket is here!"

In the next minute, Jada, Cricket, and I are surrounded by a dozen shoppers and employees, each one cooing to the poor pup about her deceased owner, and how sorry they are that Barb is gone.

Love swarms around us. My fears of being in trouble for bringing a dog into the store are long gone.

"I can't believe it," says a man I hear someone call "Gregory". He braces himself when he gets on his knees. I'm guessing he is in his sixties, because he lets out a winded "oof" when his joints creak on the way down to petting Cricket. "Barb was just over my house, telling me all about her plans for her big move." He shakes his head. "She was trying to be excited about it, but I could tell she didn't want to go." He looks up at Jada. "I mean, who in their right mind would want to leave Apple Blossom Bay?" He shakes his head. "Pete did her gutters that morning, and he refused to take a dime from her as payment because she baked him a pie. I mean, who would murder a sweet woman who bakes pies for the teenagers around here?"

Well, that crosses Pete off my list as a suspect. I'm guessing Melinda, his mother, was upset he didn't take the pie *and* the payment, then blamed his decision on Barb.

Betty gives Cricket a dog biscuit, ignoring the person in her line, who I'm guessing is an out-of-towner, like me, because she looks flummoxed to see a dog in a grocery store being fawned over.

Betty pets Cricket while my pup munches happily on the biscuit. "I still can't believe Barb's daughter talked her into selling her house and giving her and her husband the money. What would Barb have gotten out of that deal? They never came to visit. She was always the one flying out to them to see her own grandkid. Her daughter never called unless they needed something." Betty shakes her head, her permed and dyed bright blonde hair swishing over her shoulders in dismay. "Well, I never. And now she's gone. That sweet soul up and sold her home to give her greedy daughter the money."

Betty looks to be in her fifties, vivacious and filled with conversation and opinions.

I like being around people like that because I don't have to talk much. I get to blend in while still appearing sociable.

Gregory shakes his head. "Barb was going to move in

with them to basically be the full-time babysitter for the grandchild she only got to see once a year. It's a crummy way to treat a fine woman like Barb." He casts up his hand, silently requesting for assistance to get back on his feet.

Though I don't know the man, I offer my arm to help him up. "There you go."

Gregory is a good man, because even though I gave him my right arm that was born without a hand, he doesn't retract from me, but takes the help without caveat.

I don't like when people shy away from my right arm. It's not diseased or anything. Loads of people are born with symbrachydactyly.

Gregory shakes my left hand, now that he's standing. "Thank you, young lady. You one of Jada's friends from out of town?" He grins at Jada hopefully. "A new girlfriend?"

Jada chuckles. "No, Gregory. This is a new friend."

I gnaw on my lower lip before I summon enough courage to introduce myself. "I'm Emily's niece. Hannah Hart. I'm staying with my aunt for a while. It's nice to meet you."

Gregory's smile widens on his weathered face. He missed a patch shaving this morning. The gray of his partial beard is hard not to stare at. "Good to meet you. Emily mentioned she was excited to have you come out. Shoot. I would've worn my good shoes, had I known. Any niece of Em's is a niece of mine."

"Oh," I remark pleasantly, "are you dating my aunt?"

Gregory shakes his head with a smile. "No, ma'am. I

was fixing to take Barb to the next town bonfire, actually. Finally got up the courage to ask her. She must've been out of her mind, because she said yes."

Sadness widens my eyes. "I'm sorry, Gregory. Unfortunate timing."

Moisture glistens in his eyes, which seem to hold both cheer and sorrow simultaneously. He aims a crooked finger my way. "Learn from my mistake, girls. If you want something in life, don't sit back and assume the world will wait on its keester for you to get up and do something about it. When you find the thing or the person you want, go after it with all you've got."

My wrist goes over my heart. I don't know how to tell him that I would do exactly that, if only I knew what my passion was.

Or would I find my passion and do exactly nothing about it? Would I sit back because it's better to be quiet and careful than loudly make a mistake?

Mistakes always feel loud to me, so I live my life with the goal of not making waves, not taking up space, and not going after anything that might be too much a risk.

I moved across the country to start over, yet here I am, struggling with the same problems I've had all my life.

I can only hope that Apple Blossom Bay has room for me, so I can learn how to take Gregory's advice.

10

NINCOMPOOP

*B*etty hugs Jada while they talk quietly about how horrible the Barb's passing has been. Betty fans her slender face. "That anyone would hurt a sweet soul like Barb is beyond me. Do you the police have any leads?"

No good ones, I want to gripe, but I keep that little quip to myself. "They're hoping to find clues," I tell the small gathering who is still fawning over Cricket. "Any ideas on who might have wanted to hurt Barb?"

Betty answers firmly, arms akimbo. "You mean other than her daughter, who only wanted that woman for her money?"

"Other than the daughter, seeing as you might have seen her roaming about town if she was here at the time of the murder. If she lives in a different state, she might have a solid alibi that puts her miles away from the scene of the crime."

Betty's red-painted mouth pulls to the side. "I can't think of anyone else who might not have adored her. Barb made the best peach cobbler in town. She had a kind word for everyone she met."

Gregory grimaces. "Well, a kind word for people who deserved it. She wasn't too happy with the groomer she took Cricket to last month."

I glance down at the long-furred dog, amazed that she's been recently groomed when her fur is so fluffy. "Wow. Cricket's hair grows back quick if she was just groomed last month." I'll have to remember that if I get to keep Cricket a bit longer.

I try not to get too happy about that thought, though it dances in front of me all the same.

A dog of my very own. A gorgeous lovebug to cuddle with whenever I want.

No, no. Best not get attached to that idea. Life rarely goes *that* well.

Gregory shakes his head. "She didn't end up staying for the appointment. They wanted to use clippers on our sweet little Cricket here and shave her fur. I've never heard Barb get cross with anyone, but I heard that argument clear as day from the parking lot. Barb lived alone, mind you, so Cricket was her little princess." He motions to the prettiest dog in the world. "Can you blame her?"

I tilt my head to the side. "What happens if you shave a dog? Is that bad?"

Gregory holds his hand parallel to the floor and tilts it from side to side. "For most dogs, it's fine, but for a toy Pomeranian? The fur can grow back in looking all ratty, like the dog has mange. Barb brushed Cricket's fur every day. That coat is perfect because of all the care she put into her princess."

I make a mental note, suddenly realizing that just because I've always wanted a dog doesn't mean I know how to take care of one. "Oh, wow. I think I've got a lot to learn. I'm looking after Cricket until Barb's family decides what to do with her. Maybe I should get her a brush. I didn't see one sitting out at Barb's house." I turn to Betty, who works here. "Do you have a section in the store for animals?"

Betty nods. "Absolutely. Wouldn't be Apple Blossom Bay if we didn't. The dogs that live here are the town's celebrities, really. Follow me." Though she has a person still waiting to be rung up, she escorts me to the animal care aisle. "Should be a grooming brush for long-haired dogs in there. Don't bother with a normal brush. You'll need the deluxe grooming kit. That would be best for Cricket's long coat."

It starts to dawn on me that I know next to nothing about dogs. The fact that my parents wouldn't let me get a pet growing up might have been a good idea on their part.

Jada seems to sense my growing melancholy, because

she presses her palm to my elbow and walks with me to the spot where the grooming tools are clustered on the shelf. "This one," Jada rules, though she doesn't seem that much more certain than I do.

I turn to her, holding tight to Cricket's leash. "I don't know what I'm doing," I blurt out in a rush. "I've never had a dog. I've never lived more than ten miles away from my parents. I've never lived in the countryside like this. None of it."

Jada takes in my anxiety and plops herself down on the floor of the store, then she motions for me to join her.

Upon my hesitation to sit on the store's floor, Jada reminds me gently that, "Breathing helps."

I nod, pulling air into my lungs more forcefully than is helpful. Jada is patient with me while I wrestle with the idea of sitting on the floor of a public space, and the scolding that is sure to come from the store's owner.

But Jada appears so peaceful that I acquiesce after a very loud internal debate.

The two of us pet Cricket while we sit together. When Jada speaks, she keeps her eyes on the dog, who doesn't seem worried in the least that I have no experience taking care of an animal. "I'm twenty-six, and I burned oatmeal yesterday morning. Not even stovetop oatmeal. The stuff that just heats in the microwave and comes out perfect."

I soften at her confession. "Aunt Em will teach you. If you can wrangle twenty-two kindergarteners, I have faith that cooking isn't too far outside your reach."

"You left home," Jada reminds me, switching the focus to me as she motions to my forlorn face. "You can't say those things about yourself anymore, because look at you. You own a dog (for the moment). You live away from home now in a completely different state. It's a lot all at once, but you're no longer that person who 'can't' or 'shouldn't'." She chucks my shoulder as if we're old friends. Her umber eyes are kind and filled with warmth. "You're not that girl anymore, Hannah. You broke into a houseboat today." Her eyebrows dance. "You're one step away from being completely and totally out of control."

I snort at her assessment of me. "I'm sure no one has ever used those words to describe me before."

"Until today." She smirks at me. "Hannah Hart is sitting on the floor of a store. Hannah Hart has a dog—one of the best in the world, might I add." She pauses to kiss Cricket, then hits me with another wild grin. "Hannah Hart is totally out of control."

I don't know why, but I love the way that sounds. "You think?"

"I *know*." Jada glances up at the dog toys. "What would you do in your old life to unwind? You look like you've had a lot of new things hurled your way all at once."

"I do puzzles and read," I answer without skipping a beat. I do other things too, but I hardly think Jada needs to know about my odd hobby of making dog biscuits for the stray behind the gas station when she just confessed her insecurities in the kitchen.

I have a very specific cooking talent, which I have learned is non-transferrable to human food. I make boring cookies for people, dry chicken, and flavorless pasta. I don't even bother cooking my vegetables anymore because I only make them taste worse than their raw version.

But I can bake a dog biscuit that makes a pup sing.

Of course, I was only feeding a stray who probably would have preferred my dry chicken to the homemade biscuits, but I like to tell myself that my secret special talent is real, and it made that dog's world a better place.

Jada stands and then hoists me up. "Let's get potatoes and head over to the book section. Then we'll go to your place and Em can teach me how to make mashed potatoes that don't taste like glue. Your aunt is a saint, if you didn't already know. This is her second time teaching me after Phyllis gave up."

I cast around for aisle markers. "There's a book section in this place?"

"Sure is. Like the sign on the front of the store says, 'If they don't have it, you don't need it,'" she reminds me. "Everyone needs to get lost in a good book every now and then."

When Jada extends her hand to me, I don't hesitate to grab onto it. Even though we are new to each other, we walk in step through the store like twin girls looking to start a new adventure in tandem.

Though I barely know Jada, I draw solace from her

closeness. If I don't know where something is, she will find it. If I trip, she will catch me.

If I get lost, she will make sure I find myself, even if I'm not always sure who I am, or if I am worth finding.

The potatoes go into the cart she grabs, along with the almond flour, peanut butter and eggs I put into the buggy. Jada doesn't question my additions, which is good because I don't want to admit my destressing hobby that I am going to indulge in tonight so I can clear my head.

I select a paperback about prairie life, which is a genre of which I never tire. Not too harrowing. Not heavy on romance. Just right.

By the time we check out, I am hungry and ready to eat my weight in mashed potatoes.

Gregory is in line ahead of us. He chats animatedly, as if we're old friends. "You bring Cricket by, you hear? There's no dog in this town that makes me smile more than she does. That pup was born to make the world better."

My head bobs. "Yes, sir. I'm sure Barb would want Cricket surrounded by her favorite people."

Gregory crooks his finger at me again. "And no shaving that dog, or Barb would have something to say about it. Called the groomer a nincompoop, if you can believe it. Never heard her use that kind of language before. If the groomer was fired, I wouldn't be surprised. Everyone respects Barb."

I meet Jada's worried gaze as we load our things onto the belt. I can tell we are thinking the same thing.

Jada murmurs to me under her breath. "If the groomer was fired because Barb was upset, that might be cause for the ex-groomer to attack her."

I grimace. "I hate that anyone would stoop to such depths to exact their revenge."

"Me too, but it's not outside the realm of possibility."

I reach down and run my fingers through Cricket's overgrown fur. "Then I think a visit to the groomer's is in order."

Jada's eyes widen. "You think?"

I hand my card to Betty, who checks out our small bag of items while crooning affectionately at Cricket.

If I am going to get to the bottom of who could have killed an old woman in her own home, then visiting the person Barb called a "nincompoop" seems like the right place to start.

Maybe small-town life isn't as peaceful as I thought.

11

KITCHEN MISTAKES

*A*unt Em is just as patient as I remember, but the kindness is foreign to me because I haven't been exposed to it in years. Back in my childhood, Aunt Em was my Uncle Emilio. But with time passing as it has, Emily is ever the same welcoming, joyful presence.

She almost makes me believe that I can learn new things and actually try without the worry of making a mistake holding me back.

Back in the city when I was growing up, if I wanted to learn something, I would wait until my parents were gone, and then I would experiment without an audience. They have something to say about imperfections, which happen every now and then in the kitchen. All the air would go out of my sails, and I would give up before I'd even properly failed at the task.

But Aunt Em is nothing like her sister. She is only strict

about which songs should be sung while peeling potatoes, which Jada and I have no reason to protest.

"Louder!" Aunt Em shouts. "If the potatoes can't feel Dolly Parton's soul in the air, then they won't be as fluffy. Sing it like you mean it, or we'll start over."

I sing louder, even though I am not the one peeling. This is Jada's culinary quest.

I, on the other hand, am mixing the almond flour, egg, and peanut butter with a wooden spoon in a large metal bowl, filling the air with peanut buttery deliciousness.

Do I need to make Cricket a whole batch of dog biscuits? Probably not. She's got plenty of food and a small bag of treats I brought from Barb's home. No dog *needs* a batch of peanut butter biscuits, but on the other hand, *every* dog needs a batch of peanut butter biscuits when life has been this much of a whirlwind.

I didn't start baking dog biscuits until I moved out of my parents' house into my own apartment. There I had the freedom to make cautious mistakes inside closed doors.

But when Aunt Em throws a handful of chopped onions into a pan with seemingly no plan behind it, I go out on a ledge and test the outer limits of my daring. "Aunt Em?" I ask over Jada's singing. "Would you mind if I look at your spices?"

My aunt quirks an eyebrow at me before throwing open the nearby cupboard. "Hannah Grapefruit, you don't have to ask. This isn't *my* home; it's *our* home. If you see something you like, take it. If you want to move something to a new spot, do it. My only rule is that you enjoy your life here and do something good for yourself. I'm very strict about that."

I chuckle at her rigid rule.

Aunt Em holds up her finger. "It's harder than you think. I want you to do something good for yourself." She points to my mixing bowl. "Does that fit into the criteria? Plants are my thing. They make me feel fresh and new, like anything is possible. You have to decide for yourself what makes you come alive."

I swallow hard, really giving it some thought. "Baking dog biscuits for Cricket makes me feel like I'm really loving her with all my heart. Like I'm giving my best to her. Filling her with happiness fills me with happiness, so I think this counts."

Aunt Em nods to grant her approval and motions to the well-stocked spice cupboard. "Proceed."

I tiptoe over to the spices, knowing exactly what I want to use.

The turmeric is practically screaming at me, so I pluck it from the cupboard, ready to put it to use. With careful fingers, I unscrew the lid, sniffing to see how much I should use.

I really should measure things, but whenever I make dog biscuits, my heart takes over and does the measuring for me.

While Jada is singing Dolly Parton ballads to her potatoes, I wait for the turmeric to tell me how much of it I should use.

Turmeric is good for a dog's joints. Because Cricket is small but solid, I worry that her short legs might grow sore after a while from all that walking and occasional jumping up to sit with me whenever my backside hits a couch.

The peanut butter just plain smells wonderful, making me salivate just as much as Cricket for the treats.

I'm no culinary wizard. I can make spaghetti and a few boring dishes that my parents complained about minimally. But I am a whiz in the kitchen when it comes to baking for a dog.

That, or dogs are just naturally grateful for even the most boring sustenance.

After a long day, there is nothing I like more than mixing the biscuit ingredients and turning them into a sticky lump while my problems fade to the background. In fact, the longer I take, the less anxious I become. I am no longer worried that I am taking up space in my aunt's home. My left hand combines the ingredients in a steady rhythm while my right arm holds the bowl still. As Cricket sits at my feet while I stir my problems out of the way, I realize that I like it here.

I can breathe, and I don't think that is the sole doing of the ocean air.

My aunt is making space for me. Thus, I can breathe.

Aunt Em takes a break from coaching Jada through the process of boiling chopped potatoes, which, I'll admit is pretty adorable. She bumps her hip to mine and jerks her chin toward the turmeric in my hand. "That is one spoiled dog, I hope you know. Homemade biscuits?"

"That's the plan."

I expect a lecture from my aunt about not wasting my time on something we can easily buy from a store already made, but instead, she reaches down and pets Cricket. "I love it," she croons. "Follow your bliss, Hannah Grapefruit. It's the only way to live."

A smile finds me at her approval that I am free to be my weird self, even if it makes no sense. This time, when the chorus comes around, I sing along, even though I was told by my choir teacher seven times (I counted and still recall each time) that my pitch was flat, and I can't stay on the beat.

Dolly Parton doesn't care if I'm imperfect, and neither does my aunt or Jada.

So, I keep singing, finding a smile I didn't realize I had bubbling beneath the surface.

I inhale the turmeric again, noting its earthy, muted scent.

Jada's hips move while she chops the garlic according to Aunt Em's specifications. "You don't use measuring spoons. Is that how you do it? You smell it to tell how much to add?"

"Only when I'm making dog treats. I'm worried I'll ruin the batch if I'm wrong and add too much, though." I put the turmeric back in the spinning rack in the cupboard. "Best play it safe. A little turmeric is fine."

Aunt Em tugs the small canister back out. "Rule number two: 'Play it safe' is akin to cussing out a minister in this house. Anything worth doing is worth doing wrong to get it right."

I chew on my lower lip, unsure if I should take her liberating words seriously. "But I might ruin the biscuits. They have to be healthy *and* delicious, not just healthy."

Aunt Em shrugs. "If you ruin the batch, then we won't have dog biscuits for dinner." She winks at me and tosses the pan that has the onions in it, browning them evenly on all sides before she throws in more butter.

Now the kitchen smells like a dream.

In fact, this *is* my dream—making something delicious in a space where I am allowed to make mistakes.

Jada dumps her peeled and minced garlic into the sauté pan with the onions, then stands back to survey her work. She has the look of a scientist about to attempt the impossible.

If Jada can try again and again to cook, even though she claims it rarely turns out well, then I can take a chance.

Maybe I can make a mistake here.

I take a deep breath and dump not one, but two whole tablespoons of turmeric into the metal mixing bowl.

I turn the oven on, admiring the work that must have gone into painting one's appliances purple.

The smell isn't what I was hoping for, but I know I can't

judge it yet. I need to let the biscuits cook so the flavors marry before I can declare this a failed venture and dump the ruined treats in the garbage.

I can feel Aunt Em watching me while she instructs Jada to get out the masher while the potatoes cook. After I put away the spice, I turn to her, seeing true sadness in her usually jovial hazel eyes. "What's wrong?"

Aunt Em scoops me up in a hug that radiates through my whole being. "I didn't realize how badly you needed to be here. Watching you overthink adding a little turmeric to something?" She squeezes me tighter. "You need the ocean. You *need* this dog." She pulls away and bends down to pet Cricket. "And you both need me. I should have had you come out here sooner, Hannah. I assumed you'd grown up to be much like your mother—always sure of herself and ready to conquer anything, even if it doesn't need to be conquered. But you're nervous about the smallest thing." She picks up the shaker of turmeric and hands it to me. "More."

I glance at the offering, scandalized. "I already added in two tablespoons!"

"Add more just to be wild. I'm telling you; it's liberating."

I take the small jar from her hand and open the lid once more, wary and worried I am about to take this batch from pretty okay to completely inedible. "I don't know, Aunt Em."

Jada starts chanting, "Do it. Do it. Do it," over and over,

so much that Cricket barks and starts jumping on her hind legs to add more pressure.

I close my eyes and hold my hand over the mixing bowl, letting out a high-pitched nervous squeak when I shake a few sprinkles loose. Then, with a surge of boldness, I add much more.

It's on the fifth shake that the smell I was hoping for truly bursts free. Turmeric is a sneaky one, tasting like nothing until you add too much, which is usually the perfect amount.

Jada squeals while Aunt Em claps.

Maybe going too far with a non-spicy spice isn't all that bold to most people.

Those people are lucky they have the confidence to believe that a life lived with mistakes can still turn out okay.

In time, hopefully I will get there.

I mix the concoction, letting the dough do what it's supposed to, which is unwind the knots that come from a puzzle unsolved.

I want to talk to the groomer Barb was angry at and see what came of them. Did they get fired? Are they sore about being called a nincompoop?

I want to know more about Barb's family, who kept her at arm's length until they needed money, then expected her to up and sell her home so she could move in with them and be their live-in babysitter. The fact that Barb would be far from the ocean and the home she created here didn't seem to be a factor.

I want to know if Barb blushed when Gregory finally worked up the courage to ask her on a date. The blushing is my favorite part of any new encounter.

There's plenty of blushing in prairie novels whenever the handsome new farmhand rides into town.

I've never blushed like that, but I love the intrigue of it when it's laced with innocence and sweetness. My last relationship was just fine, but there was little blushing between my girlfriend and me.

I also want to know who Phyllis saw at Barb's house, wearing the brown suit, matching shoes, and the bowler hat, yelling at Barb as if he had a right to such crass behavior.

I want to know it all, including how Barb would want me to look after her dog. Cricket has burrowed into my heart, where I pray she never leaves.

Even while I work the dough in the kitchen, Cricket sticks tight to my ankles, looking up at me as if I am fascinating (which I assure her, I am not).

After an hour in the fridge, the mixture is ready to be baked. Using my aunt's cookie scoop, I dig out the dough and drop it in small plops on the baking sheet. I catch Jada cataloging my movements out of the corner of my eye. She's watching how I maneuver the baking tasks with a missing right hand, which I don't mind in the least. The fact that she doesn't jump in and try to be helpful is a welcome bliss. I don't like it when people take over when I am perfectly capable.

Jada and I get along well, for which I am grateful.

I wonder if Cricket has ever tried homemade biscuits before, or if this will be an adventure we share together.

How I want to have wild times with a dog by my side. I want to pay Cricket back for the adoration she beams at me, as if I deserve such affection.

The kitchen air fills with the comforting scent of peanut butter, and fifteen minutes later, my eyes are wide because I did it.

I tried something outside the box, unsure how it would turn out, and nothing horrible happened.

NOT ON THE LIST

*D*eputy Hanson is turning out to be one of my least favorite people in Apple Blossom Bay. When the doorbell rings the next morning and I see through the peephole that he is standing there in full uniform, my stomach tightens.

Cricket barks over and over, letting me know (in case I didn't hear the doorbell) that we have company. I lean down to pet the fluffy Pomeranian before I open the front door. "Can I help you?" I ask the officer, not making a move to invite him inside. Maybe he's just doing his job, but putting his focus on my aunt should be no one's job when the actual killer is lurking somewhere out there.

Plus, I am still in my pajamas. Gray sweatpants and a stained faded t-shirt aren't the most glamorous nightwear, but if it ain't broke...

I can only hope he is stopping by at eight in the

morning to tell us how sorry he is that he borderline accused Aunt Em of being capable of anything nefarious, which she is not.

Deputy Hanson motions to my standoffish gait. "Are you going to invite me in?"

I cross my arms over my chest, trying to look intimidating in my slouchy pajamas. "Are you going to accuse my aunt of a crime she didn't commit? Because I feel like you can do that from where you're standing."

Apparently, I *am* capable of being defiant; I just have to be defending my aunt to find my voice.

Deputy Hanson narrows one eye at me, as if to make it clear that he does not appreciate my sass. "I have some more questions for your aunt. Is she at home?"

I debate lying, but I'm not sure if that's some sort of felony—lying to a police officer during a murder investigation.

I call over my shoulder. "Aunt Em, one of your handsome suitors has come calling. What shall I tell him?"

Aunt Em's chortle wafts in from the kitchen, where she is enjoying a slice of toast paired with Phyllis' homemade jam. "A handsome suitor? Let me put on my good pearls." She trots into the living room in a fluttery blue blouse paired with white slacks. The back of her hand drapes over her forehead as she feigns a swoon. "Good gracious! A man in uniform. Just my luck."

She looks like a supermodel, especially in comparison with my oversized pajamas and messy hair.

Deputy Hanson aims his stink eye my aunt's way. "Hilarious. Can you pretend this is a serious investigation?"

"I can pretend just about anything, Benjamin. I can even pretend you weren't Captain Hook in our elementary school play." She forms her finger into the shape of a hook and lets out a swarthy "Arrr, matey!" Aunt Em bumps my hip with hers. "He was such a good villain!"

Deputy Hanson reddens but does his best to keep my aunt in the current conversation, even as she tries to change the trajectory of it just to throw him off-balance. "Yes, well, I'm here to ask if you were on the books to take that couple to Barb's house the day you found her. I don't think you were, judging by the people I've spoken with thus far. Anything you want to say about that?"

Aunt Em's angular jaw firms, but then she blows off the insinuation that anything could possibly be wrong. She fluffs her dark hair over her shoulder, looking like a runway diva fresh off a photo shoot for women destined to have it all. "Just because I wasn't on the books for that day doesn't mean I didn't have an appointment scheduled. Barb and I arranged it all on the phone. That's why you don't have a record of it. Barb is an old friend. We don't need formal dockets and whatnot."

Deputy Hanson lowers his chin as he addresses her. "You realize that looks bad, right? You were there on a day you weren't supposed to be, according to the sign-up sheet

Barb had of realtors stopping by to show her house to potential buyers."

Aunt Em shrugs, sipping her coffee, as if this entire conversation doesn't bother her one bit. "I don't know which of us is more forgetful in our old age—Barb or myself."

Well, that's untrue. I can't speak to Barb's mental acuity, but my aunt is sharp as a tack. And a woman in her mid-fifties is hardly old.

My aunt's blasé expression falls to mild frustration. "You're rude as ever today, talking to me as if I am a criminal from which the police need to protect our sleepy ocean town. Goodness gracious. With me roaming about, selling real estate to interested buyers, who knows what sorts of crimes will occur!" She feigns scandal, but then sips her coffee again, narrowing her eye at Deputy Hanson. She purses her lips. "This is because I told people that you have holes in your underwear." She spreads out her free arm as the deputy's face reddens. "If you didn't want the town to see your underwear, you shouldn't be hanging it on your clothesline!"

I snicker at the feud between my aunt and the deputy, then shrink under Hanson's unamused glare.

Deputy Hanson points his finger at Aunt Em. I fight the urge to jump in front of the gesture, so the sight of it doesn't hurt my aunt's feelings. "I need to know if you're holding any information back, Em. I don't like surprises." He shakes his head at my aunt. "The evidence is starting to stack up against you. For your own good, I'd stop being snarky and start telling me things that can actually help me take some of the heat off you."

I swallow hard as my aunt's gaze narrows with displeasure. "That'll be enough out of you for today, Benjamin. You can see yourself out."

I slam the door because it's the angriest thing I can think to do.

I don't like the idea of anyone accusing my aunt. But then again, why was she at Barb's house when she didn't have an appointment? Is that just how things are done around here, or is there more to the slip than an honest mistake?

I cling tight to the idea that my favorite aunt isn't a criminal. I want her to only be guilty of spontaneity, not murder. I lock the front door, hoping to keep any further accusations away from my aunt.

13

LOOKING AFTER AUNT EM

*S*leeping with fresh ocean air wafting in through the open windows last night was a dream come true. Even the visit from Deputy Hanson this morning hasn't managed to ruin my haze of relaxation. It's been a few nights in a row, and I'm not sure I have ever slept so soundly.

Though, perhaps I can attribute much of that solace to Cricket, who likes to sleep with her head on the pillow next to mine, tucked under the covers like a human, and cuddled in my arms like a teddy bear.

At one point in the night, she whimpered in her sleep, inching her body closer to mine.

Pure Heaven.

Going from a twin bed to a queen is like upgrading from a studio apartment to a palace. My new bedroom has two pink walls and two cream-colored walls, with a fluffy floral bedspread celebrating both hues. The stylish night-stand and lamp look like they've come from a catalog for Bed and Breakfasts. There's even a vase filled with paper flowers, made with love by Jada's kindergarteners.

After I shower, brush my teeth, and get dressed in jean shorts and a hopelessly wrinkled gray t-shirt, I ask my aunt for directions to the groomer in town.

My aunt peers at Cricket over her second slice of toast that has been generously slathered with Phyllis' jam. "Are you taking her to be groomed already? She doesn't look dirty to me."

I fill a glass with water and drink slowly. "I ran into Gregory yesterday with Jada at the Forgotten Stock Market."

Aunt Em quirks her brow at my left turn in the conversation as she looks up at me from her seat at the kitchen table. "I'm glad you're meeting new people. Gregory's a sweetheart."

"Seems like a nice man. He mentioned he heard Barb yelling at a groomer there who wanted to shave Cricket. I figure I'll go talk to them and see what came of that argument. I'm sure the groomer didn't up and kill Barb, but at this point, I'll do anything to get another suspect on the list. I have to make sure you aren't the focus of the investigation."

Aunt Em smirks at me. "That's sweet. But don't make yourself upset on my account. Benjamin won't arrest me. If I'm brought in on actual charges, Phyllis is under strict

POMERANIAN PUZZLE | 101

instructions to print out the picture I have of Benjamin's pants splitting when we went bowling last year and post it all over town." She winks at me over her mug of morning tea. "I know how to play ball."

My phone chimes with a text from my mother.

HANNAH, MAKE SURE YOU'RE APPLYING YOURSELF OUT THERE. Your Aunt Emily needs you to be on the ball.

AUNT EM MUST SENSE MY DROPPING MOOD. "EVERYTHING okay?" she asks.

I tuck a strawberry blonde curl behind my ear while I lean my hip to the counter in the purple kitchen. "When my parents told me to move out here, my mom made it sound like you needed help around the house. I've been here three days, and I haven't helped with a single thing. In fact, because I brought a dog into the house, I'm sure I've actually made more of a mess for you."

Aunt Em snorts her amusement. "My sister has always thought I needed help, but I have a good life here. When the ocean is within walking distance, a woman has all she could possibly need. Ocean town life didn't suit her when we were children, but it's perfect for me." She leans in. "But if your mother asks, I'm falling apart and can't possibly make it another day unless you're here."

I smirk at her offering of an easy out for me so I can

stay here as long as I like, but I don't know my aunt enough to be sure she's not dodging something dire. "How about your health? Do you need help with anything there?"

Aunt Em shakes her head, and I see no sense of dishonesty in her. "Fit as a fiddle." She sets down her teacup and sighs with the heaviness of someone about to deliver an unpopular truth. "Look, Hannah. The thing that's wrong with me in your mother's eyes is that I am unmarried, I tend to be a bit spontaneous, and I don't care that I'm not filthy rich. If there was a fix for that, I wouldn't want it. I'm happy. I'm healthy. I'm just glad you're here. I think she was afraid my contentment would rub off on you when you were younger, so she moved you as far away from ocean life as possible so she could give you the tools to become an overachiever. That's a good life for some, but it's not right for everyone."

My shoulders sink as reality dawns on me. "And now she's given up on me achieving anything of value, so she sent me here. I'm not here to help you out," I realize as my self-esteem sinks lower than I can scoop it off the floor. "I'm here because I failed, and my parents are ashamed of me."

Aunt Em doesn't agree with me, nor does she brush aside my verdict. Instead, she spreads her arms out wide. "Welcome to Apple Blossom Bay, my dear. It's where the misfits fit in just fine."

I snort. "They should put that on the 'Welcome to Apple Blossom Bay' city limits sign."

She stands and kisses my forehead with a short embrace after she sets her dish in the sink. "Never mind your parents' expectations. That's a bar no one will ever reach—not even them. Who do *you* want to be?"

I fidget with the hem of my gray t-shirt, unsure of the answer to that.

I've never known. Not really. When my parents selected business school for me, I hoped (along with them) that a passion or direction would surface, but it never did.

In fact, cuddling Cricket is the most alive I have ever felt in my life.

I'm not sure that qualifies as having a purpose.

I swallow hard. "I'm not sure."

Aunt Em smiles and curves an arm around my shoulders, squeezing me gently. "Good. That's the perfect place to start. It's okay to be a bit lost every now and then."

"What if I never find my path?" I ask meekly, voicing my very real worry. "What if I'm always lost? Or what if I choose a path and it ends up not being the right one? Then I've wasted all that time, just like I did with business school."

Aunt Em shakes her head and then stands straighter, her chest puffed out. "Start by doing something good for yourself, sweetheart. Find a spark of happiness and follow it until it shines into a guiding light."

"You really think it's that simple?" I quip, knowing it is anything but.

Aunt Em kisses my temple, infusing me with a warmth

and acceptance I cannot create on my own. "If you want to find yourself, you will. Amazing girls like us generally get what we want."

I chuckle at how very wrong she is, but I decide to savor her words of wisdom.

If I want to find myself, I will. I have to start on that path by doing something good for myself.

I wonder how true that is as I toe on my old sneakers and set out to explore the town for the day.

14

PUZZLES AND PINS

I am out of my element in this town, but I'm grateful for the change of pace. Back at my parents' house, if someone had been suspecting me of murder, it would be the all-out panic attack until things were set straight. But looking at my Aunt Em, one would never guess she is the least bit concerned. That doesn't stop me from taking these allegations seriously, though.

After feeding Cricket and brushing her luxurious fur with the wire brush (that apparently, she hates but tolerates well enough with a few disgruntled chuffs), I get out the leash and take her for a walk. While I am still unfamiliar with the lay of the land, I navigate with my phone well enough to take me through the main thoroughfare of the town. I wish Jada was by my side, explaining the town to me while we walk together, but she works during the week, so today I'm on my own.

Accompanied by the best dog in the world.

We pass an indoor fish market, where Cricket leads me inside so she can beg for a sardine from the owner, who greets her by name with an indulgent smile.

Smart girl.

We walk by a comic bookstore called "Adventure Walkers", which also sells walking shoes, oddly enough.

Then we pass a bakery that smells like a chocolate chip cookie haven. My pace picks up, so I am not tempted to start my day with a bucket of cookies.

There is a jigsaw puzzle and quilting store called Puzzles and Pins, which sounds like a good place to lose myself for a few hours. I've always been a sucker for puzzles. I decided to leave my collection behind at my last address because I didn't have a ton of room for extra nonessentials in my car.

I peer into the picture window, staring at a sign that reads "Join our Puzzle Exchange Program".

Before I can remind myself of my mission to speak with this dog groomer, I am strolling into the store, making sure to ask the person at the register if I am allowed to bring my dog inside her place of business.

My dog, not *the* dog. Though I know in the back of my mind that I am simply caring for this pup in the interim while Barb's daughter decides what to do with her, my heart knows where it belongs, which is with my precious Pomeranian.

The red-haired, smiley owner of the store greets

Cricket by name and waves us inside. "Good morning, ladies!" she says to Cricket and me. "I recognize the dog but not the owner." She tilts her head to the side, her wavy shoulder-length hair swooshing away from the nametag that reads "Vivian."

I pretend Jada is beside me, making me braver and more vocal while I shake Vivian's hand. "I'm Hannah Hart, Emily's niece. I'm staying here for a bit, so I thought I'd make myself useful and look after Cricket while Barb's daughter makes arrangements."

Vivian lowers her chin. "So terrible. Barb was here all the time. She was a puzzler. One of the best."

"A puzzler? You mean a person who likes to do puzzles?"

Vivian nods, motioning to the sign that drew my eye on my walk. "She was a proud member of the Puzzle Exchange Program. Went through at least a thousand pieces a week."

I lean down to pet Cricket, who sits pleasantly as if she has no further agenda than to enjoy the day, wherever it takes her. "Puzzle Exchange Program?"

Vivian takes a card from her register and hands it to me. "For ten dollars a month, you can rent puzzles from the store. You can do as many as you like throughout the month, just so long as you rent one at a time. Take a puzzle home, finish it, bring it back and take another." Her red eyebrows dance with mischief. "It can be quite the addiction. Most of my puzzlers take out one a week, but it's unlimited, really. Whatever a person needs in life, a puzzle tends to help them get there." She pulls out her phone and displays the screen to me. "You can take a picture of the finished puzzle, send it to me, and I'll post it on our website. Sort of a time capsule of your puzzle conquests."

Every sentence Vivian says to describe this club is better than the last. It's this introvert's dream come true, really. A store filled with puzzles that I can rent out as needed for one low price? A new puzzle whenever I need it?

I lean in to peer at Vivian's phone, noting her vanilla perfume that invites me to take a deep inhale. As she scrolls through the puzzles listed, I see a series of names beneath of the many people who have completed each one. "Oh, that's incredible." Though I am trying to keep money in my pocket, being that I have a mountain of student debt and no job at the moment, I find myself taking out my wallet because if there's one thing I love, it's a good puzzle.

Perhaps that's what is drawing me to solve Barb's case. I don't have all the pieces yet. I need to know how they fit together.

The other side of the store seems to contain all the bits and bobs for sewing and crafting, but puzzles are where my heart lies. There is a backroom in between the two halves of the store, but I stick to the puzzle wall, where I decide to take my aunt's advice and do something good for myself.

Though it might be a small thing, joining the Puzzle Exchange Program is the start of me putting down roots here. I'm choosing bliss over the boredom of never measuring up.

I love puzzles, so I decide to lean into the thing that brings me joy.

After I fill out my form and hand in my ten dollars, I feel the thrill of possibility. Vivian marches me to the wall of puzzles, where I can select any box I want.

The colors and pictures are overwhelming. My mind is reeling while goosebumps stand on my arms. If there is a heaven on earth, it is this place. And I have my dog at my side to experience the joy with me as I take it all in.

"Are any of them speaking to you?" Vivian asks from my left, her hand motioning to the wall of puzzles that stretches from the floor to the ceiling. There is even a sliding ladder attached to the shelves to reach the top row.

My brain works overtime to take it all in. "I want to do them all! I can't decide."

Vivian chortles at my flabbergast. "They're divided by shelf for how many pieces are in each puzzle. So, for example, this shelf all the way across is all the five-hundred-piece puzzles. The next one up is one-thousand pieces. Then as you go across, they go by theme. So here are nature scenes. These ones here are of Apple Blossom Bay, you know. Then these are animal themed, and on it goes."

My mouth falls open because it's not just that this is the perfect subscription club for me; it's that it is also organized immaculately. "I think I'll try a five-hundred-piece puzzle for now. Build my confidence before I jump to the sweet spot of a thousand pieces."

Vivian nods and motions to the corresponding shelf. "Here you are. Barb stuck with five-hundred-piecers for years before she ventured to the thousand-piece boxes. She had an affinity for the puzzles that were pictures of Apple Blossom Bay." Her upper lip curls. "Horrible people, her family. Wanting her to sell her home and give them the money. It's not the thievery that's the worst of it; it's the fact that they wanted to take her away from the bay. This place was her life. She loved it here. What's a woman like Barb going to do in the city?" She shakes her head, clucking her tongue to make her disapproval plain. "Poor Barb has a puzzle at her house still." She bats her hand. "Not like that's the thing to focus on."

I turn to Vivian, centering myself when Cricket licks the outside of my leg. "Which puzzle did Barb last turn in? I'd like to check out that one, please. If I'm watching her dog, then I'd like to do her puzzle."

Vivian's hand goes over her heart. "I think that's nice. I'll grab it for you." She moves down the row and selects a puzzle that has a picture of the harbor not too far from here.

My mouth falls open as my pitch climbs. "That's the fish market! I was there yesterday with Cricket and Jada." I'm so proud of myself for being able to recognize a small part of the town.

Vivian smiles indulgently at me. "That's right. Barb took Cricket there every Saturday without fail. Such a lively spot. Plenty of things for a dog to investigate." Vivian sniffs a few times like a curious pup, which makes Cricket bark twice.

Gosh, I love her cute little barks.

Vivian writes down my puzzle of choice in her ledger, then bids me farewell.

I wasn't planning on picking up a puzzle, but after moving my possessions across the country and setting up my new life on the day I discover a dead body, I think an evening with a puzzle is just what the doctor ordered.

Though, as I start my journey to the groomer's, I know I will not be able to sleep tonight unless I retrieve the missing puzzle from Barb's house so I can return it for her.

15

BUBBLES AND BARK

*B*eing surrounded by yips and barks is a joy I did not discover when I lived in the city. I love the happy puppy energy, the smell of dog biscuits at the register, and the cute canine things for sale at the pet groomer's store called Bubbles and Bark.

The urge to buy outfits to dress Cricket in is strong, but I fight it as best I can, since I currently have no source of income.

The woman at the front desk greets me with a smile that is weighted with busyness. Her high side ponytail rocks to the left when she looks up at me. "Good morning. Welcome to Bubbles and Bark. How can I help you?" She rises from her seat a few inches and looks over the edge of her desk. Immediately her voice turns syrupy. "Hello, Cricket! I didn't think I'd see you here so soon." She comes around the desk and crouches down to give Cricket a proper snuggle. She's wearing calf-high neon pink boots to match her lipstick. "You poor baby. I heard about Barb." She looks up at me as she kisses Cricket's maw. "Are you watching Cricket?"

"Just until the family decides what they're going to do with her."

The woman stands and extends her hand. "I'm Xiuying. It's nice to meet you. I admit, I was worried about Cricket when I heard Barb passed." She shudders. "So horrible."

I nod, loving the way Cricket circles to my side to let Xiuying know that she loves me most.

It's a heady privilege, to be loved by a dog. I didn't earn the love. I didn't do anything but wake up and feed her, yet she clings to me as if I am someone special.

I clear my throat. "I stopped by to see if Cricket is due for a grooming. I don't want to drop the ball looking after Cricket while I have her in my care."

Xiuying's hand goes over her heart. "That's mighty nice of you. I love that you're taking that into consideration. Regular grooming is so important." She flips open her appointment book and trails back a few pages. "Well, she was bathed two weeks ago, but she didn't get a trim. We had a newer groomer we were trying out that week, but Cricket didn't take to her. I can schedule you for next Friday, if you like. That's my earliest opening."

"What happened to the other groomer?" I ask casually, though I know bits and pieces.

Xiuying leans in and lowers her voice. Perhaps since we look to be around the same age, she trusts that she can tell me her secrets. "She was new to grooming. Didn't study the nuances. Different breeds need different care. She shaved Mrs. Dennings' prize-winning poodle when Mr. Noodles came in for a nail trim and a bath. I had to let her go after that. Turns out, she only knew that one haircut: a shave with the clippers. Sometimes that's the way to go, but you have to discuss it with the owner first. And not all breeds take well to that. Their fur can grow back coarser after it's shaved, like our Cricket here. We would never consider using clippers on her." Xiuying shakes her head as she recalls the memory. "Barb nearly lost her head when she heard the clippers buzzing after she brought Cricket to us not too long ago. I've never heard that woman raise her voice, but Cricket was her baby, understand." She smiles sadly at Cricket. "I'm glad to see Cricket ended up with someone who cares about her just as much as Barb did. Checking to see if she needs grooming?" Xiuying gives my knack for hyper-focusing on the details a thumbs-up.

I put my name down for a grooming on Xiuying's Friday availability in two weeks. "I might need you to walk me through proper care of her," I admit. "To be honest, I've always wanted a dog, but this is my first one. I didn't know Barb, but I don't want to disrespect her by not caring for Cricket the way she would have wanted."

Xiuying rounds the desk again, and this time, she throws her arms around me. She looks eons lighter than I feel because she smiles more effortlessly. "I'm so glad to hear you say that. I'll give you my cell phone number. You can call me night or day with any dog questions." She taps her heart when she pulls back from our embrace. "All the dogs in Apple Blossom Bay are like my nieces and nephews. I want to see them loved, living their best life. Please don't hesitate to call me for anything." She jots down her phone number and hands it to me. "You're Em's niece, right?"

"How'd you know?" I'm still reeling from someone giving me their personal cell phone number and telling me I can bother them whenever I feel like with dog questions. I cannot fathom anyone from the city being that open and welcoming.

Xiuying bats her hand at me. "Em's been telling everyone who will listen how excited she is that her brilliant niece is moving in."

I tap her number into my phone and then glance up at her. "Hey, whatever happened to the person you had to let go? Was she mad?"

Xiuying holds her hand parallel to the floor and tilts it from side to side. "I mean, she wasn't thrilled to be fired, but I offered to pay for her to take a class at the grooming school in the city half an hour west. Once she takes that class and demonstrates that she learned enough for me to trust her to groom the dogs in this town, she is welcome to come back."

My mouth pops open. "That's really generous of you."

Xiuying shrugs as if it's all no big deal. "I'd rather she learn than go somewhere else and ruin those dogs' beautiful coats."

I push further into the gossip, needing just one more piece of the puzzle. "Do you think she was angry that Barb yelled at her?"

Xiuying tilts her head to the side, her high black ponytail swishing to the right while she considers my question. "I can't imagine anyone is happy to be yelled at. She cried in my office, but Barb stayed until she came out. She apologized for losing her temper, and that was that." She leans in. "It was actually Barb's idea to have her take that class. We're of the 'teach a woman to fish' school of thought, rather than 'break the fishing pole when you make a mistake' types of people." She points to the bench for visitors near the check-in desk. "Barb sat with her right there until she calmed down. Then Barb took her out to lunch. They had a nice time, I think. She came back to the shop all excited because Barb taught her about Cricket's coat, and how best to care for it."

I love that that's how conflict is handled in Apple Blossom Bay. If only the rest of the world could adopt the same kindness. "I'm glad they were able to work it out. Sounds like there were no hard feelings between them."

Xiuying shakes her head. "Oh, no. No one can be angry with Barb; she's too nice."

I am glad to be able to cross the scorned dog groomer off my list of suspects. Though, that means I am back to square one, which is trying to figure out who on earth could possibly have killed Barb.

I know it wasn't Aunt Em. I only have to prove that to the police before they narrow their investigation on the wrong suspect.

FLOWERS

*A*fter our long walk, I decide to stop by the house for lunch. My heart drops into my stomach when I see a hastily scribbled note on the counter from my aunt. "At the hospital. There's potato salad in the fridge for lunch."

I am getting quite the education on the ins and outs of the major landmarks in Apple Blossom Bay, and now I am about to learn where the hospital is located.

I take Cricket into the backyard for a bathroom break and then skip lunch so I can get to my aunt at the hospital. My mind is racing, wondering what could possibly have happened that landed her in the hospital in the two hours I was away from the house.

I was sent here to look after her. I knew there had to be more to this than my mother being embarrassed about my aunt's unmarried, spontaneous lifestyle.

Maybe she has cancer.

Maybe she has some other scary disease.

I didn't press hard enough. I didn't make her tell me all that was going on. What should I do when she gets back? Will she need a wheelchair? Will she need memory help or movement assistance?

I panic when I should be planning, but then I quickly realize I won't know what to plan for until I get to the hospital and talk to the doctor. Then I'll know what it is we are dealing with.

I kiss Cricket and then explain that I will be back in two hours or less. I hug her on my knees because I need the comfort.

My aunt is the liveliest family member I have. She makes me laugh.

She cares if *I* laugh, which is a gift I have needed my entire life.

I grab up my purse, lock the door and get into my car, driving at the top of the sluggish speed limit so I can get to my aunt as quick as possible.

The hospital on the outer edge of Apple Blossom Bay is small, even though it appears to serve two towns. There are only three floors and one giant parking lot. I waste no time securing the first spot I see.

Horrible possibilities flip through my brain, reminding me that I know precious little about my own flesh and blood. I don't know what makes Aunt Em laugh till she cries. I don't know her favorite food. I don't know her favorite sad movie.

Purple, my brain tells me, throwing me a bone. *You know her favorite color is purple. That's something. Or it's the beginning of something, and you'll build on that.*

Plants, my brain reminds me. *She loves plants. They make her feel alive.*

I race into the hospital, breathless when I reach the front desk. "Excuse me, I need to find my aunt. She said she was here. Emily Burton. Can you tell me where she's been taken?"

The nurse quirks her brow at my harried nature. "Em? Sure. She's in the pediatric unit. Just that way."

My stomach is in knots. I need my dog with me, but pets aren't exactly allowed in a hospital, I'm guessing. Cricket would calm my nerves while my family member is in crisis.

It doesn't dawn on me until I am halfway down the hallway that my mid-fifties aunt with zero children has no reason to be in the pediatric ward.

Maybe they ran out of beds in the regular part of the hospital? I have no idea.

I follow the signs until I get to the pediatric unit and have to check in at their desk.

I scribble my name, answering quickly when the woman asks who I am here to see. "Emily Burton. My aunt said she was here. Is she okay?"

The nurse smiles at the mention of my aunt's name.

"She might be low on balloons, but I'm sure she'll make do."

My nose scrunches. My mind goes from gastric balloons to gift shop balloons, wondering what the nurse might mean.

The nurse waves me to a room on the right. "She's in Room 312. You can go on in, but you have to wear a mask."

I take a paper mask from the box on the desk, pop on a visitor's badge and rush to the room in question.

I take a breath before I slowly open the door, ready to be my most compassionate and attentive self. If Aunt Em didn't want me to know she was sick, I am resolved to be gentle with her pride when the truth finally comes out.

This is why my parents sent me here.

But the scene unfolding in the hospital room is nothing I was expecting. In fact, I have no frame of reference for the clown standing in front of me, nor the child in the bed, who is clapping for the entertainer.

My Aunt Em's voice greets me from behind thick white makeup and an exaggerated painted red mouth. "Oh, good! I'm glad you found me. I'm running low on balloons."

I gape at my aunt, taking in the scope of her clown costume that is covered in fake flowers of all varieties and colors. She has enormous purple shoes on her feet and a purple, curly wig under a straw hat with a frisbee-sized purple flower on the brim.

"What are you doing?" I ask her, unsure if I have gone

crazy, or if perhaps she has. One of us has clearly lost touch with reality.

"I'm Flowers the Clown," she explains, as if I should have guessed as much. "But I got a papercut this morning, so my balloon-tying hand isn't up to snuff. Don't judge me on my work today."

I step forward, taking the tube-shaped balloon in my hand while my flabbergast washes over me. "You're Flowers the Clown? And you're at the hospital because..."

She motions to the child in the bed. "Because I heard there was an amazing kid here, and I had to see for myself. Turns out, the rumors are true. The coolest kid in the world is sitting right here in this very bed!" She turns to the little girl, who is beaming with pride at being labeled the coolest girl in the world. "Shelly, this is my assistant, Hannah Grapefruit." She holds up her finger. "Do not call her Hannah Banana. She hates that."

The little girl claps, even though there is a tube hooked to the back of her hand. "Hannah Grapefruit, can I have a hat?"

Aunt Em takes the balloon and starts twisting the thing like a professional until the yellow balloon is in the shape of a hat. Then she takes out a purple balloon and pumps it with air. After she ties it, she twists that into a large flower that sort of looks like a purple daisy. She fashions that to the hat and sets it atop Shelly's bald head.

The little girl has big eyes and an even grander smile. "Thank you, Flowers! I love it! Do I look like a fancy lady?"

Shelly turns her little eight-year-old head this way and that, posing for us.

"The fanciest!" Aunt Em rules with undeniable certainty. "In fact, when the doctor comes in here, I'm sure she will say the same." Then my Aunt Em sits on the side of Shelly's bed. "Did I mention today that I'm proud of you? I heard that you were sweet to the nurses, even though you had a rough day yesterday."

Shelly leans forward and hugs her favorite clown.

If I thought my emotions had a workout on the way here, it is nothing to the swell that expands in my chest at the sight of this little girl clinging to her favorite clown.

17

FILLING YOUR SOUL

My eyes are damp when I exit Shelly's hospital room after my aunt reads the girl a book and makes her a balloon mouse to keep her company. "That's what you meant when you wrote you were going to the hospital?" I swipe at my eyes. "I thought you were hurt!"

Aunt Em's hand finds its way to my back. "I'm fit as a fiddle, hun. I come to the hospital every now and then to put on little shows for the kids here. Did you like the hat I made Shelly? It matches mine." She flicks the brim of her straw hat.

I gape at her, overwhelmed and without a shred of decorum left. "Who *are* you?"

Aunt Em chuckles at my flabbergast. "I'm just what the doctor ordered. That's who I am." She motions to the row of rooms. "These kids are all in need of a little cheer. If life was kinder, they would be outside, enjoying the spring air and the sun on their skin. Haven't I told you that it's important to do something good for yourself?"

I nod, gob smacked.

"Well, this is good for me. I get out my clown costume and come in here to practice my balloon-bending skills. I'm getting pretty good."

I sit down on the floor in the hall of the pediatric ward, giving my heart a moment to settle. "I need more information. Is this a program you're part of?"

Em shakes her head as she sits beside me, slowing her cadence so I can keep up. "About two years ago, I was searching through my closet for something to wear, and I realized all my clothes were boring. I didn't have a clown costume."

I snort. "That's quite the oversight. I mean, a person *needs* a clown costume."

I say it like a joke, but Em nods with all sincerity. "Right? I knew I needed to get one. I mean, what's funnier than a clown in a fish market? But when I put it on, the whole purpose came over me. It was easy. Like breathing. So, I went to the dollar store and bought all the balloons they had. I took them to the hospital and started doing little shows for the kids. It's the best audience, really. They're very forgiving if my balloon dog turns out looking like a mouse. It's great fun, Hannah. Whenever life gets boring, I've found that a clown costume is the perfect remedy."

I gape at her, trying to put together the pieces that make up the puzzle that her mind is to me. "I thought you were hurt," I argue. "But you were here being sweet to kids?"

Aunt Em smiles, sitting back in her seat. "I was being sweet to myself, too. Their smiles fuel mine. One day it's going to dawn on you that doing something good for your soul is as necessary as breathing. When life begins to suffocate you, it's time to change course." She motions to her attire. "In my case, I needed to buy a clown costume."

I scrub my hand over my face. "I don't know what to say."

Aunt Em sighs dramatically. "Are you about to give me a lecture about behaving like an adult? Because I get those from your mother on a regular basis."

I shake my head. "No. I'm about to ask you to teach me how to make balloon animals, so I can join you one of these days. This is really what you do? Is it your side job?"

Aunt Em shakes her head. "They don't pay me to do this. It's not a job. It's my hobby. It makes me young. Fills my heart. You can only run for so long when your heart is on empty."

I mull over her wisdom, tucking it in my pocket for a rainy day. "I think my heart was born on empty," I admit in a quiet voice. "I'm always so worried about doing the right thing, about getting everything perfect. I don't even know what fills my heart. I make a lot of mistakes, so trying new things has never been all that successful for me."

My Aunt Em lets my words sit in the air without batting them away or brushing them under the rug. "What is success?"

I open my mouth and then snap it shut because I know the words that come out of my mouth will be from my parents, not from me. "I'm not sure."

Aunt Em bops the outside of her knee to mine as we lean against the wall in the hall of the hospital. "What about that deep breath? Ever get that soul-filling, frown-breaking hearty inhale that makes you feel like you were suffocating before that moment found you?"

I gnaw on my lower lip, knowing exactly what she is describing. "Cricket fills my heart. I knew it the first time I saw her. Every time she looks at me, I feel..." I trail off, but then come back with more honesty. "I *feel*. That isn't something I let myself do all that often."

Aunt Em reaches over and laces her fingers between mine. "Maybe your mother thought I needed you to straighten me out, but perhaps you need a little of this." She motions around to indicate the life she has built in Apple Blossom Bay. "It's not a bad thing to discover that you want to live your life, Hannah. If Cricket makes you smile, then chase that. If you think dressing up like a clown for kids who need a boost might fill your heart, then that's what you need to do." She squeezes my hand. "Your heart matters, Hannah Grapefruit. You can't ignore your most vital organ."

I lean into my aunt, resting my temple to her shoulder.

I am not a cuddler, but perhaps that is because the opportunity was not there growing up. Maybe I secretly am snuggly and prone to hugs. I got a hug from Xiuying just this morning. Maybe it's this place.

Or maybe it's me.

Maybe I am coming alive in ways I did not anticipate.

She kisses the top of my head. "Benjamin called. Said if you wanted to stop by Barb's and gather the rest of Cricket's things this evening, that's when the movers would be by, packaging up her belongings."

"That seems fast. Barb only just passed."

"Life is fast. Don't forget to live it, little grapefruit."

I hold tight to my aunt's hand while life slowly unfolds itself, introducing me to possibilities I did not know could happen for someone like me.

18

SHIVER

My aunt and I make plans for her to teach me "ballooning" as she calls it, later in the week. While clowning might not be the thing my soul craves, it's a new adventure that promises to push me far outside my comfort zone, so I am going to give it a try.

When I get home, I let out Cricket and then cuddle my dog. I content myself brushing her fur while she sits on my lap and licks my face on the couch.

If there is a better life than this, I do not know it.

Loving a dog can't possibly be my life's purpose. That's not a thing.

Is it?

Because I am alone in the living room while Aunt Em showers off her clown makeup, I talk freely to my dog. "I think this is going to be good, Crick. I need a new start. I need... something. Tonight, we're going to head to Barb's to see if you have any other things in the house that you might like to keep. Remind me to pick up the puzzle that was on the dining room table. If Barb is anything like me, it will bother her even in the afterlife if she has a puzzle checked out that did not make its way back to where it belongs."

Cricket licks my nose, as if she agrees. She even holds eye contact with me when I talk to her, because we truly are best friends. Every time she kisses my cheek, I get that deep inhale of contentment that Aunt Em described.

Maybe I don't have a true purpose for my life, but if the idea is to do something good for myself, then this dog is it. Being near her, being loved so unconditionally—even if I make mistakes—is a shiny gift that keeps unwrapping itself for me.

After I finish brushing her fur, I sit down with Aunt Em at the kitchen table. I need to get my head on straight, and something tells me that the woman my mother thinks is entirely backwards might be the only person who can help me make a plan.

Cricket whines and nudges my leg with the top of her head, so I lift her up and flatten her stomach to mine, her front paws on either side of my neck. I love her little head rested against me, and the snuggle I didn't even have to ask for before it was volunteered to me without caveat.

Aunt Em brushes her dark hair while we sit together, her game face on. "Okay, niece of mine, let's do this. You want to start a new life here? Tell me how I can help make that happen."

My hand moves slowly over Cricket's fur. "Since it's clear you don't need dire help like my parents thought, I need a new plan for my time here. I want that deep breath feeling you described. So far, it's this dog. Does that count?"

Cricket nuzzles her muzzle between my shoulder and my jaw, cuddling into my neck as if I am her safe place.

"Absolutely!" My aunt gets out a piece of paper and a purple pen. "First on the list: Time with Cricket."

I snort at the suggestion. "Naturally. But also, I need to like, get a job and contribute."

Aunt Em chuckles as if I've told her I want to eat lizard brains for dinner. "Sure, sure. That will come. You haven't been here a week, Hannah Grapefruit. Give yourself some time to explore. You need to breathe. I do it habitually, and I'm telling you, it's fantastic."

I cast her a wry look. "Sure, but while breathing, I should be working."

Aunt Em shakes her head, setting her list on the table. "No. I'm putting my foot down. You will take a week or two at least and be aimless. Purpose will come to you when you're ready for it, but you can't go through life borrowing other people's expectations and calling them your plans." She pulls Cricket onto her lap when my dog turns her head toward my aunt. "Find your purpose first, then we'll figure out how to make money off it."

I mull over her words, wondering if life can really be that simple.

When the pitter-patter of rain hits my ears, Aunt Em's face lights up. "Perfect!"

I tilt my head at her. "That's usually not what people say when a sunny day turns rainy."

Aunt Em stands and grabs her phone from her purse, plunking out a text to someone. Then she rubs her hands together after setting down her phone, jerking her chin toward the front door. "I've been waiting for it to rain ever since you came back. Do you have sandals? Any sort of footwear you don't care about?"

I purse my lips. "I've got a pair of flipflops you're welcome to borrow."

My aunt's posture is erect as she bobs on the balls of her toes. "Well, hurry, then! Grab your sandals and let's go! My car's already packed."

"Packed for what? Did I miss something?"

"You're about to if you don't get moving. Hurry!"

As the rain picks up, I begin to question my aunt's hold on sanity. Regardless, I follow her lead and race to my new bedroom, where I am still not fully unpacked. I leaf through my suitcase and locate my pair of old flipflops that have certainly seen better days.

I slip them on and trot out to my aunt, who hands me a rain-proof blue poncho. "Put this on, quick! We don't want to miss it. This is going to be a short rainfall, I can tell, not a deluge. But it'll work."

I do as she tells me and race out the front door on her heels. She is surprisingly spry on her feet, as if she hasn't aged a day since I last saw her when I was a little girl. I leave Cricket in the house, because I have no idea what I am about to walk into.

It felt much like this, I recall, chasing after her whims with a nauseous feeling in my stomach that I later recognized as joy. Aunt Em has that way about her—that ability to push you over the edge and make you laugh while you dive headfirst into the unknown.

She explains nothing to me as she throws her body into the driver's seat of her purple Jeep and shoves the keys in the engine. "You ready to get a little crazy?"

I blink at her with wide eyes. "I mean, aren't we already doing that? You were just in a clown costume! What are we even doing?"

Aunt Em's eyebrows dance with mischief. "I texted Jada while you were getting your sandals on. She'll meet us there."

"Where?" I am mildly exasperated that I have no idea where we are going, or what we will be doing once we get there. A girl like me can only handle so much spontaneity before I start requiring some answers or like, a fainting couch.

Aunt Em opens her mouth but then closes it and shakes her head before speaking. "It'll be better if you don't know. You're a worrier. Sometimes it's best to buckle up and enjoy the ride."

I harrumph good-naturedly at her, but don't press her further for answers she clearly does not want to give. Even though not knowing where we are going itches at my skin, I bite my tongue and keep my multiplying questions to myself.

Back with my life before Aunt Em, I knew everything scheduled on each day well into the next month. If it wasn't on the schedule, it didn't happen. I don't know what to do with impulsivity like this. My stomach feels queasy.

My blue poncho makes crunching noises as Aunt Em speeds through the city, driving away from the main thoroughfare to the outskirts of the bay, far from any hint of suburbia.

"Um, aren't you supposed to stay in the city?" I remind her. "I'm pretty sure I heard Deputy Hanson say something like that." I sit on my left hand, keeping myself tightly wound because I have very little frame of reference for my Aunt Em's whims.

My aunt's smile is stretched wide across her face. "You look smashing in your poncho. And Benjamin will be fine with me going just a few miles outside of Apple Blossom Bay. He might even be sore I didn't invite him along."

"Along for what?"

Aunt Em doesn't answer. She merely shakes her head to let me know that I have no need for answers to things like, "Where are you taking me, you crazy lady?" She giggles as she drives, letting the raindrops hit the windshield as if it's all a game she has been waiting to play.

I wish I laughed as often or as freely as she does. I'm guessing if that is ever going to happen, I'll need to relax the tight hold I have on myself.

I start with my shoulders, lowering them just enough to allow my chest to expand and contract more easily. Then I take in a deep drag, somehow still able to smell the ocean even though the windows are rolled up.

I love that salty scent, and the freedom that comes with it.

I lean back in my seat as my aunt turns her chin to smile at me. "You did it. You're relaxing. Good for you, little grapefruit."

I smirk at the nickname of which I never tire. No one is playful with me; they know I'm not fun.

But maybe I can be fun. Maybe I can try that.

Maybe I'm not stuck being the way I am if it makes me unhappy.

When we reach our destination ten minutes later, the rain is still coming down, but there is no sign of lightning or the crashing of thunder. It's a pleasant rainfall, but when Aunt Em parks the car on the grass near the top of a hill, I don't see any buildings, other than a lighthouse at the end of a long pier.

"That's a nice lighthouse," I comment, guessing that she wanted me to see the lighthouse in the rain for some reason. Maybe it looks different like this, though I would imagine it would be nicer to see the structure on a clear day.

Aunt Em gives me a distracted "Mm-hm", but then springs into action when Jada's blue clunker pulls up next to our car. "Let's go!"

"Go where?"

But there is no chance I will get an answer out of her. She is already out of the car and opening the trunk.

I get out to help her with whatever she is struggling with, making sure my poncho is pulled over my head. "What are we doing?" I ask over the pelting sound of the rain. But when my eyes fall on the things she tugs out of the trunk, my mouth pops open. "You brought sleds? You don't mean..."

Aunt Em's hazel eyes sparkle with the joy of the reveal. "We are going mud sledding in the rain, my dearest Hannah Grapefruit."

Jada slams her own trunk shut and meets us behind Aunt Em's purple Jeep. "Nice weather for sledding, isn't it?" she says with a grin. She is wearing jean shorts and a brown-and-yellow checked t-shirt underneath a clear poncho. Her box braids are tucked into a blue bonnet to keep the rain from messing her hair too much. She is barefoot, as if she completely understands that the spring rain means it's sledding time. She needs no further information or coaxing.

Em grins at Jada. "Do you think our city girl is ready for small-town life?"

Jada grins. "One way to find out!"

I take the sleds from my aunt, utterly flabbergasted. "Mud sledding?"

Aunt Em nods. "If we don't roll around in the mud every now and then, we might be in real danger of becoming stick in the muds, which is no way to live. That's scientific fact. Like an old proverb or something. It's got to be." She points to the edge of the hill. "Shall we?"

Jada is already racing to the top of the hill, which is a gentle incline on one side, and more drastically sloped toward the ocean on the other.

A thrill of a memory mixed with the unknown races through me in the form of a shiver.

Aunt Em trots by my side up the hill. "The best things in life usually come paired with a chill down your spine, just like that one. If you feel that, then you know you're on the right track."

I don't think it through. I don't question the logic of the steps I take toward the edge of the hill, nor the rain that feels like a thousand prodding pokes from invisible fingers, urging me to wake from the sleepy haze through which I have been walking.

I don't wait for my aunt to go first. I don't even wait for Jada to set her sled down beside mine. I know that if I don't go now, I never will.

The scent of the ocean is entirely new to me when it is combined with the rain. I feel different, somehow changed in a way that will stay with me longer than the usual pep talk I often use to try and instill courage in my bones when I find myself severely lacking.

My sled hits the patches of grass on the edge, and even though I have not gone sledding since I was a little girl with my aunt (on snow or on mud), my body remembers the drill. I keep my eyes on the lighthouse, willing it to chase away the unsightly spots on my psyche I have never been able to shake. I bite down on my lower lip and sit on the red saucer that was most certainly manufactured for children.

Jada squeals behind me while Aunt Em chants my name over and over to build suspense. Though Jada doesn't know me particularly well, I must be giving off such a strong aura of change that she wants to watch the magic of this small town transform my soul in real time.

I'm going to chase that thrill of a shiver and find myself on the other side of something new.

Something wild.

I take in a deep breath, keeping my eyes fixed on the lighthouse even as I scoot myself forward.

The slide over the edge is slow at first—a silly little scootch that seems innocent and unimpressive. But when the saucer hits that first slick of mud, the speed doubles, and then picks up even further.

I didn't think to measure the slope of the trip downward. I didn't gage whether or not we were too high for my liking or if the angle of the hill was too steep to keep my bones from breaking before the end. I force my eyes to stay open. There's a scream of glee on my lips as I race down the hill through the rain.

I hit another slick of mud, and suddenly, I am flying. Like a bird shot from a cannon, I am speeding through the air, not knowing how or when I will land. The air whips over my skin, letting me know that I am the thing that nature recognizes as one of her own. For all the stops and starts of my life, this moment is one that keeps me weightless, as if I never had a worry powerful enough to stop me.

Though I am new to laughing, for at least this moment, this is who I am.

And I love it.

When I crash down onto the base of the hill and slide a few more feet toward the ocean's edge, I can only stop the saucer by tumbling off to the side.

I figure sliding into the ocean is a bad idea, since I don't know how to swim.

For several seconds, I don't move. I simply stare up at the gray clouds, letting them shift above me at their own pace. The rain hits my face, letting me know that I am very much alive, though I haven't felt the thrill of living in years.

Aunt Em calls down to me—half overjoyed and halfway panicked I might have broken something. "Hannah Grapefruit! Are you okay down there?" She has to shout, I realize, because it was such a long ride down.

I remain supine in the mud, shocked at my daring. Even as I lift my arm to give her a thumbs-up, I am shocked that the mud-soaked hand belongs to me.

My parents would throw a fit if they saw me filthy and reckless like this.

A smile takes over my features, because finally, I decide that I am allowed to make mistakes and be messy.

In fact, I am allowed to be a mess, and still I am loved.

19

CRICKET'S PINK BLANKET

After we take our much-needed showers, I get out the leash and take Cricket to Barb's house after the rain lets up. I now know the way to Barb's without having to use my phone to guide me. Though it's a long walk, I crave the time to clear my head and process the wild afternoon that left mud in my ears and lightness in my spirit.

I still have the thrill of the mud and rain in my soul, even though I have scrubbed them from my body. The clouds have parted, and the late afternoon sun is shining, warming me through when I was shivering the entire way home from the mud hill.

When I get to Barb's house, I spot a moving truck out front. Two men heft Barb's couch from the porch to the back of the truck.

I trot to the house, flagging down the movers. "Hey, I

was hoping I could get inside and retrieve the puzzle Barb borrowed. Might that be possible?"

One of the men waves me off. "Sure, sure. The police took the crime scene tape down. We were instructed to move the large pieces of furniture and donate them. Any valuables are going to the family. There's an appraiser in there now. If the puzzle isn't valuable, then you can take it. Ask him."

I trot into the house with my head ducked out of respect to its former owner.

"Sir?" I say to the man in a camel-colored suit. I hold the leash tight in my hand, but other than that, my body is completely at ease after my encounter with the mud hill.

Cricket barks four times at the man, which is more than her usual friendly yip. She growls, which is unlike her, so I tug her closer to my side. "Shush, baby. It's okay. He's supposed to be in your house."

When the mid-height, wiry man turns around from his spot near the mantle in the living room, he quickly puts down the angel figurine I noticed when I first came into the house earlier this week. "Good evening. I'm Samuel Wilton. I was sent here by the family to evaluate Barb's things to see what can be resold. How can I help you?"

"Barb borrowed a puzzle from the Puzzles and Pins store. I thought she might have wanted to return it, so if it's okay with you, I'd like to gather it up and take it back for her." I try to be assertive in my request but also polite.

The man waves off my wish. "That's fine. I'm sure no

one wants to touch that puzzle now, though. It was on the table when she died. Might want to put that on the box so the next person has a fair warning."

I straighten my khaki shorts when I realize how casually I am dressed in comparison to his proper attire. "Also, I'm taking care of Barb's dog. Is it okay if I look around for more of Cricket's toys? I got a few things when I was here earlier this week, but if there are any other dog items, I'd like to take them to help Cricket transition into life without her mommy."

Cricket's growl is low in her throat. I have never heard that sound from her before.

The man quirks his brow as if it is curious that anyone would want to put that amount of thought into the care of a dog.

"Fine, but I need full approval of anything that leaves this house. Can't have anyone trying to swindle poor Barb."

I nod seriously, feeling the prickle of sweat that often accompanies my stress when it starts to spike. I wonder if my worry that feels like test anxiety when an adult looks at me crossly will ever fully go away.

I rush to the back room, glad to be out of Mister Wilton's sight. "Okay, Cricket. We have to be quick. Is there anything here you might like to keep? Any toys? Any blankets?"

Cricket sniffs around Barb's bedroom, which is now missing the bed and the dresser. It makes me sad to think of a person's things being donated willy-nilly with no care as to whom they will go to. But I suppose that's how it is with the nature of a person's belongings. You can't take it with you, and in the end, it's just stuff.

I move to the closet, searching the floor for any toys that might belong to Cricket, but nothing stands out in the empty hollow. "Anything you care about in this room?" I ask again, but Cricket is too busy sniffing the floor because Barb's bedroom looks and feels different without a bed in the center.

We make our way to the next room, where Cricket leads me to her dog bed. I did not see it before with the obstruction of the furniture. There is also a knitted blanket that she whines at before biting at the edge to flip it up over her head. Then she shakes it off and bites the edge again, repeating the routine before she crawls into the dog bed contentedly.

Gosh, I love this sweet dog.

The second bedroom has a single bed for guests and a desk that looks like it has been used for crafting. There is a bag of yarn on the floor beside it, and some glue and scissors atop the desk with a few pieces of scrapbook paper beside a photo album.

While the people out there are sorting monetary valuables, I realize that Barb's true valuables are in this very room—her dog and her photos.

Without asking permission, I sit down at the desk while Cricket brings her blanket and rests atop my feet. I wipe my hand and arm off on my shorts to make sure I don't get any smudges on Barb's beloved photos.

I can tell she cares about her memories, because from the first page, I see the attention to detail she has put into each collage. There are colorful papers and stickers placed thoughtfully around the scrapbook. The entire album seems to be themed around Cricket.

A smile spreads across my face as images of my sweet baby dressed up for all occasions greet my vision.

This is what my soul needs.

There are holiday-themed shoots, most of which look like they were taken either in the house or at the fish market. There is Cricket in a turkey costume for Thanksgiving, an elf hat with a bell on the end for Christmas, an eight-legged fuzzy black spider for Halloween, a flower cape to celebrate the springtime, a rainbow costume for pride month, and a strawberry hat, which I'm guessing was just for fun.

I love everything about this. I glance over the edge of the desk and tell Cricket, "We are not leaving this house without your costumes. Dressing you up is going to be my new hobby, I hope you realize."

Cricket yips twice, wagging her tail at me, which I take to mean she consents to being my new doll.

I flip to the next page, which features a picture of a smiling Barb dressed as a cowgirl, complete with a Western-themed hat, boots, and a plaid blouse. Cricket is beside her in front of the fireplace in her living room, dressed as a horse.

"Oh!" I am unable to handle the cuteness.

My heart was a non-issue before I moved here. But now I feel the unfamiliar swell all the time. "It's you," I tell Cricket, sealing my fate as a woman whose purpose now somehow includes dogs. "You're the one who's made me come alive. I hope you enjoy being slathered with more kisses than you can stand, because I have a feeling that when I start dressing you up, I won't be able to stop. Brace yourself for innumerable fashion shows, you little cutie."

Perhaps if I ply her with unlimited homemade biscuits, she won't mind the funny hats and costumes.

Cricket rolls over onto her back atop my feet, the ham, letting me know that she is here for whatever hijinks suit my fancy, so long as we get to be together.

I'm guessing the photo book that is entirely of Barb and her dog will be of little value for resale. "Your new family might like this. I'll save it with your things so they can take it when they come to get you."

I try not to let that make me too sad. It's not happening today, so I don't want to despair about the fact that my time with Cricket is temporary.

I pick up the photo book and a tennis ball that I find under the guest bed, and take them to the dog bed, where I make my little pile of canine treasures.

I take the collection to the dining room, where Cricket

follows me, dragging along her pink knitted blanket that I'm sure Barb made.

While the body has been taken away and the floor scrubbed, the puzzle pieces that littered the table when I found the body are still scattered across the surface.

Being that I have an affinity for puzzles, I have to make sure that each of the one thousand pieces are accounted for. It takes time, but I know that anything worth doing is worth doing right. If I return a puzzle missing a handful of pieces to the store, I may as well have not made the trip at all.

The movers do their thing while the man in the living room continues evaluating what is trash and which things are potentially a treasure and can be resold by the family.

I make piles of one hundred pieces, so I don't lose count, and finally reach the end, which stops at nine-hundred-ninety-nine pieces.

My heart sinks. "Oh, Cricket. We're missing one piece of the puzzle. Just one. Help me look?"

Cricket has no idea what she is being helpful with, but she barks twice to let me know she is all about volunteering her services.

I get down on my knees, feeling my way around the floor in search of the last piece. "Come on, now. It's got to be here somewhere."

Cricket and I search every inch of the dining room, but there is no sign of the puzzle piece.

I hate giving up, but I know a lost cause when I see it. I

leave the dining room and search the house until I find a box of Cricket's costumes, which I know will need to come with us.

When the gentleman appraising Barb's things lets me know the movers are coming for the dining room table next, I can see that my hour of searching has come to a close.

I gather up the pieces I have into the box and put it with the dog things, then shove them all into a large trash bag.

Samuel Wilton straightens his light-brown suit as we stand in the living room beside the fireplace. He examines the items with an edge to his narrowed eyes, as if I might be trying to steal from Barb under the guise of caring for her dog.

When the man touches Cricket's blanket, my dog barks over and over until the man puts it down. Then she growls low in her throat, stating to the room in no uncertain terms that this is her blanket, and no one is welcome to touch it without her permission—especially not Samuel Wilton.

His thin upper lip curls as he pulls back his hand and rests it atop the empty mantle where a few knickknacks used to be. "Are you finished? Because Barb's daughter and son-in-law will be here tomorrow to collect the valuables and deal with the rest of Barb's things. I have a lot of work to do, and I prefer to do it without fear of being bitten."

I swallow any acerbic retort I might want to give the man as I nod meekly. "We're leaving now."

Samuel Wilton points to the front door, as if I don't understand where the exit might be.

I respect Cricket's wishes and let her carry the pink blanket out of the house after we are cleared to leave with our meager contraband.

After we make it three houses down, I stop our progress and kneel to pet Cricket. "I'm real sorry, but I think I should carry your blanket. Is that okay? It's going to drag in the mud this way, and I don't think you'd like me washing Barb's scent off it. Can I carry it for you? Would that make you angry?"

Cricket yips happily at me, as if she has never been cross with a stranger in her life. She wags her fluffy tail and kisses my face. There is no hesitation nor hint of a growl when I take the blanket from her. I make sure to keep it in plain sight sticking out of the trash bag in case she gets nervous if she doesn't know it's nearby.

The walk home is slow and burdened with many things for me to carry, but I am grateful for the time to clear my head as I think of all the plans and happy times Barb had with her dog.

I can only hope Cricket's next home will be just as happy as her first.

20

SIX HUNDRED DOLLARS

That night, Aunt Em roasts a chicken while I do the easy work of assembling a salad. We sit together at the table with Cricket warming my feet and munching happily on one of my homemade dog biscuits.

She doesn't seem to mind the extra turmeric one bit.

Aunt Em stabs at her salad. "I think we should go swimming tomorrow after you give Cricket to her new family."

I keep my head down. "Hmm." I don't have the pep in me to explain that I don't know how to swim, and I have no interest in learning this week. Nothing feels like it will ever be cheery again after I give up this perfect dog.

I can't even hope that Barb's daughter and son-in-law won't want to keep Cricket, because I know that's not in the realm of possibility. Who wouldn't want to have this dog around? She's perfection.

"I went to Barb's house this evening to pick up the last of Cricket's things. They're all packed up by the front door, ready to go."

"All except the tutu," Aunt Em remarks, smirking at me because underneath the table, Cricket is dressed in a pink ballerina costume.

"I couldn't resist." My chin lowers further. "It was the most fun I've had in ages. Maybe ever, Aunt Em. I didn't know it could give me that much joy. I feel like my heart is coming alive just in time to break forever."

Aunt Em reaches across the table and rests her hand atop mine. "Oh, honey. I'm so sorry." I can tell she is struggling to find the right words to say. "Tonight, Cricket gets chicken. A feast fit for a ballerina." She stands and moves to the cupboard, pulling down a third plate. She takes half her chicken and sets it on the dish, then slides the meal under the table. "Last night with her favorite girls? We do it up right. Chicken for all."

I offer up a wan smile. "There was an appraiser at the house when I got there, valuing all the things. He didn't think the album Barb put together of Cricket's photo shoots was worth anything, but I thought it was amazing. Want to see it?"

It's a question I would never ask my parents. Looking at something just for fun? Looking at multiple pictures of a dog? Over dinner, no less?

Never would have happened.

Aunt Em claps with cheer. "Of course! My favorite dog dressed up in different costumes? What's not to love?"

I trot to the pile of Cricket's things by the front door and pull out the scrapbook, grateful that Aunt Em isn't precious about dinner time needing to be a formal affair.

I plop the book onto the dinner table and turn to the first page.

My aunt laughs aloud at the picture of Cricket dressed as a watermelon. "Oh my gosh, I didn't think she could get rounder, what with all her fur. That's adorable!"

We flip page after page until we get to the one with Barb in her cowgirl outfit with her miniature horse, Cricket.

"Oh, we have to pause on this one for a minute. Look at how happy they are!" Aunt Em points to the two cuties standing in front of the hearth in Barb's living room. Then she fans her face, as if she needs to air-dry her imaginary tears.

My eyes brush over the details, taking in the scene that is now almost familiar to me, after being in Barb's home more than once.

I point to the mantle. "Huh. There are two angel figurines here in the picture. When I first came to Barb's the day I moved to Apple Blossom Bay, there was only one. Its arms were in a hoop that looks like the other angel fits into." I tilt my head to the side. "I wonder what happened to the other angel?"

Aunt Em shrugs. "I've never had the patience for knickknacks. You have to dust them, and if one breaks, the collection looks all sad—like an angel hugging the air."

I slide the photo out of its pocket to examine the back. "Looks like Barb must have lost the angel in the last week or two, since this was taken three weeks ago."

Aunt Em frowns. "Three weeks ago?" She shakes her head. "I hate thinking of recent memories when my friend is dead. It's like she's still here, but not. Makes me sad."

I scoot my chair beside Em's so I can hug her while we eat. "I'm sorry you lost your friend."

"Thanks. Me, too."

When an idea occurs to me, I am out of my seat in the next breath. I grab my phone and do an image search on the foot tall angel in the photo, after I take a picture of it.

"What are you up to?" my aunt asks me, craning her neck to see my screen while she munches on her chicken.

"Maybe I can track down the missing angel and replace it for Barb. She doesn't care now, I mean, obviously, but the angel should have its buddy. A sort of thank you to Barb for getting to spend this week with Cricket."

Aunt Em doesn't judge my irrational heart that breaks for a ceramic angel, and a woman I never knew. "That's nice."

But my bright idea falls when I see the steep price tag for the small gesture. "Six hundred dollars?" I exhale dejectedly. "Well, I guess we'll go with the thought instead of the gesture."

"It's the thought that counts," Aunt Em reminds me kindly. "Six hundred dollars for the pair?"

I shake my head. "Just for one. Its mate is another six hundred."

"Woo! That is a commitment. Good for Barb. Spend your money on something that makes you happy."

"But she lost the other angel."

Aunt Em shrugs. "I think she's too busy hanging around real angels now to be bothered by something like that."

"I guess you're right."

I go back to my meal but pull Cricket onto my lap after she gobbles up the last of her chicken. She is my absolute favorite ballerina. She licks my chin because she knows I am down in the dumps.

Cricket will go on to live a happy life with her new family, but I will miss her terribly.

21

TRESPASSER

*B*eing new in town is a nicer treat than I thought it would be. Everyone is friendly and happy to greet me. They assume they will like me, it seems, because they love my aunt. I really appreciate this kindness by proxy. Maybe I didn't need to worry that I wouldn't be accepted.

Maybe I don't need to worry at all.

When Jada called me up this morning to see if I wanted to help her with a project for her kindergarten class, I didn't hesitate. After getting Cricket ready for a longer walk, I kissed my aunt's cheek and headed out the door with the cool morning air hitting my face.

I don't know when Barb's daughter will want to pick up Cricket, so I decide to go about my day as if this isn't the last time I will see this wonderful dog.

As if the whole thing doesn't break my heart.

I am proud of myself because I only get turned around once on the way to Jada's houseboat.

I don't know how to announce myself once we arrive. It seems rude to just step onto the boat without letting her know I'm here. There isn't a doorbell, and her door would require me getting onto the boat's platform itself to knock on it.

I mime knocking in the air from my spot on the dock, then call to my friend through the closed door, which is several feet away. "Jada?"

When no one answers, I size up the divide between the dock and the edge of the boat. When there were stairs connecting the two, the journey from point A to point B was wobbly but doable. Now I'm not so sure, since I don't see the stairs lying around.

Also, the houseboat seems to have drifted, because there is a two-foot gap between the dock and the lip of the houseboat's platform.

I awkwardly lower Cricket down but take a few steadying breaths before I attempt the feat myself. I put a sailor hat on my cute dog today, thinking it the perfect accessory to wear on a houseboat.

I turn and lower my body, aiming for the edge of the boat's platform, so as not to step on Cricket. My furry friend seems to want to venture to the exact spot I am trying to move to, no matter how many times I adjust to a new spot. I don't want to step on her face, but she won't move to the side.

I lower my foot halfway between the dock and the houseboat when a man's voice startles me. A deep command calls to me from inside the houseboat. "No trespassing!" the man booms.

I jerk my body, scared that I will be arrested for trespassing when I was sure Jada told me to come here this morning. I shriek when I lose my balance, my body wobbling when a man opens the front door of the houseboat, his eyes wide. "Steady!" he calls.

But it's too late. My leg moves one way and my torso jerks in the opposite direction. "Ah!" My foot misses the dock completely, and my body plunges off the pier, dowsing me in cold water that quickly closes over my head.

I scream underwater, my arms flailing because I haven't the faintest idea how to swim. I push myself up the second my legs kick into gear. My mind stammers with ideas of what it might feel like to swim, but my muscles won't cooperate beyond frantic flailing.

With a giant push—either from my legs or from the ocean, I cannot tell—my head breaks the surface of the water just a few inches from the edge of the houseboat.

I splutter incoherently while I try to grab the edge of the platform, but I can't get a grip on the thing that is too slippery to grasp.

The man who was in Jada's house leans over the side and casts down a rope to me. "Grab on and I'll pull you up!"

I don't recognize him, and for a second, I wonder if I dropped my dog onto the wrong houseboat, but that is neither here nor there when I am trying not to drown.

I grip the thick rope and hold on tight while the man drags upward, finally reaching out his hand to clasp my wrist.

"Easy does it! Don't worry; I've got you."

I shriek because I don't know this man, and the first time I see him, I nearly drown because he assumes I am a trespasser.

Still, the stranger pulls me onto the boat, lowering me to the floor while I catch my breath.

Cricket laps at the water on my cheek, as if that is the thing this situation calls for. She barks twice, unsure if I was in danger, or just playing a fun game where I got to splash in the water.

The man kneels beside me, his brown eyes staring into mine. "I'm sorry!" he frets. "I thought it would be funny to scare you. I don't know why. You're white as a sheet."

"Where's Jada?" I ask him, confused as to how this whole situation unfolded. Drops of water blink into my vision while I shiver. "Isn't this her house? I'm not a trespasser, I promise!"

The man nods. "Jada ran to the store to grab a few things. I was supposed to let you in."

I cough in his face, my body shivering from both the chill and shock. "Who are you?"

"I'm Niles, Jada's brother."

"Hannah," I mutter. "Hannah Hart." As soon as my vision clears with a few more blinks, my breath stills in my lungs.

Niles looks to be a year or two older than I am, and with the same rounder jaw and kind eyes as Jada's.

Before I can stop my brain from turning into mush, I realize that Niles is the handsomest man I have ever seen in my entire life.

His curly black eyelashes, imploring gaze and sturdy, muscular frame are enough to turn me into a complete idiot. I grasp for anything that might resemble words but come up short.

Though doing so gets his jeans wet, Niles sits beside me until I catch my breath. "I really am sorry. It's usually a lot more fun to harass my sister's friends. I didn't realize you would fall overboard in the process."

I try to speak but delve into a coughing fit all over again.

Niles sits me up to slap me on the back. It takes me a few beats before I gather my gumption enough for words to spill out.

And wouldn't you know, they're all the wrong ones. "You scared me! I don't snow how to swim! I could have drowned!"

Niles' brows raise. "You don't snow how to swim?"

I shake my head in a sharp, jerky motion. "You know what I mean!"

"I snow what you mean." The corner of his mouth

quirks with amusement at my verbal slip. "You really aren't from around here, huh. I wouldn't have let you drown. I pulled you out, didn't I?"

My chest heaves as I take in the scope of him, unable to hold back my obvious ogling. He looks like he might have played sports in high school—muscular from neck to toe. "Niles? Jada has a brother? I'm not trespassing?"

Niles shakes his head, fighting with a smirk. "Not even a little. Man, I really scared you. It was supposed to be funny, but now I forget why. And you were worried you might drown?" He pets Cricket with regret radiating out from him. "Blue eyes," he breathes, confusing me so much that my nose crinkles. Then his eyes widen with surprise that he spoke those words aloud.

"Cricket's eyes are brown," I correct him.

"They sure are." Niles clears his throat. "You want a towel?"

I hear Jada call to us from the dock before I can answer. "Hey, guys. Oh, good. You've met." She looks down on me from the dock as she approaches. "Why are you wet, Hannah?"

I jerk my thumb at Niles, whose neck shrinks as he stands. "I met your brother. And then the falling. I drowned, but I'm okay."

Yes, words have deserted me. I should never be allowed around attractive people who make my stomach flip.

Niles casts his sister a hapless smile. "I might have scared her and made her topple overboard."

Jada covers her mouth with her hand, shifting her purchases to tuck under her arm. "Niles, you fool. Can't you just let my friend into my house without incident?" She shakes her head at her brother. "Come on inside, Hannah. I've got clothes you can change into."

Niles helps me to stand, but he doesn't release my hand right away. "You okay?"

I nod, gulping under the weight of his concern. He is a good two inches taller than I am, but he carries himself without the need to lord his height over me. "Towel?"

"Sure thing." He trots inside while Jada takes a wide wooden plank from the dock and slides it over the water, connecting the space from the dock to the raised lip of the boat's platform.

Well, I could have done that.

Jada hops down into the boat, clucking her tongue at my soggy state.

"So, I met your brother," I tell her, stating the obvious with a glower.

Jada chuckles at my wet clothes. "I can see that." She waves me inside and points me to the bathroom. Niles hands me a towel on the way, and Jada knocks on the door a minute after I step inside to hand me sweatpants and a tank top.

"I'm heading out," Niles says loud enough for his voice to carry. "If you need me to scare you into the water again, let me snow, Hannah. Nice to meet you." Then I hear a smirk in his voice. "Hannah Hart."

I grumble as heat climbs in my cheeks, but now that he is leaving, my flustered nature doesn't appear to be long-lasting.

"I'm glad you're here," Jada says when I come out of the bathroom in her clothes. "A weekend without crafts is a waste, in my opinion. How are you at drawing straight lines?"

Cricket wastes no time scurrying to me once I move into the main area of the cabin. She barks twice, wagging her tail because she is all about arts and crafts, too, if it gets her out of the house and around the people she adores.

"I can draw a straight line," I tell Jada. "But fair warning: my artistic talents end there."

Can I draw a perfectly straight line? Maybe, but I might make a mistake.

Jada gives me a thumbs up and points to her kitchen table, which is covered with posters of various colors. "I'll take it. I'm making a board for my students that shows them how well they did in trying to meet their reading goals. Every book they read they get a star."

"You need me to make a graph?"

"Yes. That would be perfect. Then I can work on the proactive kindness poster over here."

"The what?" I tilt my head to the side, sizing up the stickers and cutouts that have yet to be glued into place.

"It's a list of things the kids can do to be proactively kind to each other. On Monday, we are going to push in all the chairs for the first graders after they finish their lunch period. That's one thing. The kids are going to help me make a list of more ideas we can do to help the people around us."

My hand goes over my heart. "That is the sweetest thing. You're a good teacher." I sit down at the table and grab up a pencil. "I remember learning the alphabet. I remember being told to color inside the lines, but other than that, I don't recall much of kindergarten."

Jada blows a loud raspberry while she lays out her pink posterboard on the floor. "Color inside the lines? No thanks. We skipped that lesson in my class. The proactive kindness lessons are more for my own sanity, really. I just know that if I see one of my kids in a few years and they're being a jerk, I'm going to punt that kid into the next county."

I snicker at the mental image as I draw the first line all the way across my blue poster board. "So, the proactive kindness is more to keep you out of jail."

Jada points at me. "You got it." She lays out a few of the cutouts that are in the shape of stars over her poster. "How is Cricket doing with you and Em?"

"I wish I could keep her forever. That's how well it's going. Barb's daughter is flying in now to sign all the papers for the sale of the house and deal with what's left of the estate." I keep my eyes on my work, so I don't reveal my broken heart. "I have to give Cricket up today if Barb's daughter is ready for her. She'll go home with her new family."

As if Cricket understands me, she whines. Maybe I am projecting, but it sounds like she is saying she wants to stay with me.

If only that were enough.

These past few days of having a dog have been the best of my life. Maybe that's because they've been combined with Aunt Em's lively energy.

Jada makes a sad cooing noise. "I'm going to send out my most fantastic hope that Cricket gets to stay with you forever."

I hold tight to my pencil. "That's the dream, but that sort of miracle isn't the kind of thing that happens to me."

Jada tilts her head to the side. "Maybe that used to be true, but you live here now. Anything's possible."

I shake my head. "I'm grateful to have had the time with Cricket while it's here. I've got all her stuff packed up to send with her new family."

I am trying to keep my voice even and stoic, but misery has not left my side since I awoke this morning.

"I'll miss Cricket," Jada supplies. I can tell she is trying to draw out my sadness, so I don't wallow in silence. "I think everyone here will. There are a lot of people with dogs in Apple Blossom Bay. The dogs are little celebrities. Most of the store owners keep a stash of dog biscuits at the ready. There are very few businesses that won't allow pets in their stores. Most of the time, the dog is greeted before the owner." She motions to Cricket's attire. "I'm glad you dressed her up. I love that sailor hat. Very fitting for a day on a houseboat."

I nod, trying to keep my melancholy at bay. "Me, too. She's the most perfect dog I've ever seen in real life." I draw another line on the poster. "I'm glad you asked me to come over. I need the distraction."

Jada nods. "I figured. I'm going with you to the dog exchange, too, by the way. When you get the call that Barb's daughter is ready, I'll meet you there."

My head lifts so I can stare at her. "You will?"

Jada nods with certainty. "Of course. What are friends for? I'm not about to let you go there by yourself. Cricket deserves a proper sendoff, and you're going to need a hug and a friend after you say goodbye."

I set down my pencil and leave my chair so I can hug the wonderful woman. My arms tighten around Jada, and she doesn't hesitate to return the affection. "I never had a close friend who would go with me when I had to do something hard, just to be there for me."

Jada rubs my back. "Well, you can't say that anymore, can you."

We work side by side, finishing the two posterboards Jada needs, and then we make small gift bags for a classroom celebration she is throwing in a few days.

When my phone chimes with a text from Aunt Em, my stomach sinks. "Aunt Em received a call from the deputy requesting Cricket come to Barb's house now."

Jada's spine straightens, bolstering me the best she can with her bravery.

I am a ball of emotions. My stomach twists in such a violent knot that I worry I might throw up.

My soul feels crushed under the weight of losing someone so precious to me. These are my last moments with the dog of my dreams.

22

BARB'S DAUGHTER

*J*ada puts the leash on Cricket, then links her arm through mine while we take the long walk from her houseboat to Barb's home. We should drive, and Jada offers to take us in her car, but I don't want to speed anything along. In fact, in my habitually punctual life, this is the first time I have ever purposefully been late for anything.

But when we arrive arm-in-arm with Cricket at my side to Barb's house twenty minutes late, no one seems to notice.

The house is devoid of all furniture, leaving no place to sit. The front door is open, so we walk in and call through the house. "Hello?"

A woman in her forties jogs out of the backroom. "Are you from the auction house?" She narrows her eyes at our casual attire, as if she questions the integrity of the auction house if they employ vagrants such as us.

Whatever. I'm dressed for a stroll, not a day on the job.

"Actually, I'm Hannah Hart." When my name and the dog at my side don't ring a bell, I explain further. "I've been watching Cricket. Are you Barb's daughter?"

She nods and shoves her hand out for me to shake. She recoils when she realizes the hand she means to shake doesn't exist, and it's clear she doesn't feel comfortable gripping my wrist.

She wipes her palms on her stomach with a grimace. "Hildy, yes. Right. I'm supposed to deal with the dog stuff. The officer told me you would deal with the dog. Why is it here?" She looks down with her upper lip curled at Cricket and then shivers. "Ugh. Dogs dressed as humans is my pet peeve. I thought you were taking it to the pound. Isn't that what you do?"

I blink at her, unsure how our wires got so crossed. "Actually, I've been dog sitting until you came here. Then you were going to take the dog with you. Did I get that wrong?"

No, I didn't get it wrong. That is what the deputy explained would happen.

Hildy shakes her head. "It's been an eventful week, Anna."

I don't bother correcting her on my name, but Jada isn't shy. "It's Hannah, not Anna."

Hildy harrumphs. "I have no idea what I told the officer the day I found out my mother died. But as it stands now, there is no way I can take the dog with me. I have a baby, who probably doesn't want to have a hand bitten off by a mutt."

I gape at the woman, my hackles raising.

Before I can speak, the appraiser walks in, briefcase in hand. Samuel Wilton's hair is slicked back with hat hair, his shorter, wiry frame clad in a brown dress shirt that matches his shoes. "Here it is, Hildy. I have the receipt from the items we sold for you, plus one item that needs your signature. Perhaps we can go over it together."

Hildy nods, ignoring me as if I have been unceremoniously dismissed. The two walk into the kitchen together, leaving Jada, Cricket and me speechlessly standing in the doorway.

Jada speaks out of the side of her mouth. "Um, does that mean you get to keep the dog?"

I shrug. "I have no idea. What just happened?"

Jada elbows my side, a tiny squeal squeaking from her lips. "You caught a lucky break. I vote we take the dog and make a run for it!"

I smirk at the swell of relief from the stroke of good fortune.

That never happens to me.

The urge to take my win and run is strong, but I need Hildy to say that I am allowed to keep Cricket. I have to hear the words come out of her mouth, otherwise I will worry I might be dognapping.

I wander into the kitchen while the man is going through the list and showing Hildy the check for all she is getting from the sale of her mother's things. His briefcase rests on the counter while he slides out several forms.

"That's great. That will help so much," Hildy says. "Then after we sell the house, we'll have all we need."

I chew on my lower lip, trying to figure out a way to be conversational about intruding into an interaction that has nothing to do with me. "Did you end up getting a good price on the angel figurine? I looked it up last night and saw it was worth six-hundred dollars."

The man's spine stiffens. "I don't know what you mean. There was no angel figurine."

I frown at him. "Sure, there was. The one on the mantle that was missing its mate."

Hildy turns to me. "That's right. I couldn't believe my mother spent that much on a pair of ceramic angels. Six hundred apiece. Can you imagine?"

I jerk my thumb in the direction of the living room. "There was only one when I was here last week. She must've lost the other."

Hildy's mouth presses in a tight line. "Just a few weeks ago. Mom told me about it. Some guy tried to buy it off her, but she wouldn't sell it. Then he invited himself over for tea, and the next day, it was missing." Hildy shakes her head. "I can't believe someone would steal a knickknack."

Samuel takes a step back. "Yes, well, it wasn't here, so there's your check for what I was able to sell for your mother."

I look down when Cricket starts to growl at the man. She loves everybody. It's odd to see her territorial over me, putting her body between mine and Samuel Wilton's.

I lean down to pet Cricket. "One of the figurines was sitting on the mantle when I found Barb's body."

Hildy checks the itemized list of things sold. "Huh. It's not on the list."

The man shakes his head as he pulls his briefcase to his chest. "No, it wasn't here. Are you calling me a liar?"

I guess I am, but I'm not bold enough to say so aloud. "I just know what I saw."

Jada's upper lip curls at Samuel. "And I know what I see." She motions to his form. "There's the liar right there. I'm a teacher. You think I don't know when a lie hits the air right in front of me?"

Samuel shakes his head at us. "I'll be going."

I take a step forward, blocking his exit. "Barb's things were moved yesterday. I didn't realize your company did such quick turnarounds," I comment, suspicion rising in my bones.

Hildy turns to me. "The estate people were scheduled before my mother passed. She was selling all her things to prepare for the move, since she was going to come live with us. But she would never sell those angels. She loved those things, and she was crushed when the mate went missing. She was going to bring the angel she still had with her to New York when she moved in with us. That's why the man who wanted to buy them was so angry—because she wouldn't sell either one." Hildy scoffs. "What a loser. I can't imagine who would care that much about a stupid toy."

The man's nostrils flare. "I'll have you know that this particular brand of angel figurines is priceless if they are signed by the artist. Worth far more than six-hundred dollars. Certainly nothing stupid about them."

I gape at the man as Jada slowly moves her body to stand in front of mine. She crosses her arms over her chest. "Excuse me?"

I speak slowly, my heart pounding in my ears. "You know what kind of angels they were? You know how much they were worth?"

Samuel's eyes widen but he tries to hold his decorum. His nose lifts into the air. "I'm an appraiser. It's my job to know."

I shake my head, finding my voice in between Cricket's livid barks. "But you said they weren't here. How would you know what kind of angel figurines they were?"

Samuel stammers his reply, but it is too late for anything to undo the conclusion I am racing toward.

I am breathless as my words hit the air. "It was you. You're the one who came here to appraise Barb's stuff for her moving sale. You're the one who came back and invited yourself in because you wanted the angels."

Cricket's growl seals the man's guilty verdict in my mind. Now I know exactly who killed Barb, and I know the very poor reason why.

23

THE MISSING PUZZLE PIECE

*J*ada stares down Samuel Wilton, serious and menacing as she crosses her arms over her chest. "You were in Barb's house before she died, appraising her things for her move. When was that?"

Samuel shakes his head as he backs into the counter in the kitchen. "I'm sure I don't know what you're getting at. A lot can happen in a few weeks. Do you know how many people have been in and out of this house?"

Hildy's intake of breath is coupled with a nod in my direction, letting me know that her mother's phone call complaining about the lost angel fits into that timeframe.

I take a step around Jada toward Samuel, my finger aimed at him while Cricket growls at my side, pulling on the leash. "You appraised Barb's things for her move, and you saw the two angels. The first one went missing around the time you paid Barb a visit to evaluate her things to sell for her move." I gage the size of the angels from memory. "But you could only sneak out one discreetly. They're a foot tall. You came back for the other when you were supposed to be appraising her things to sell off after she passed."

Jada's nostrils flare. "You killed Barb! Why didn't you take the second angel the moment you murdered her?"

The man's jaw ticks. The house is empty, so when he casts around for something to attack me with, he finds nothing of much use. "I don't have to explain myself to you!"

Jada's voice is sharp but thick with emotion. "You killed Barb!"

"I would never!" Samuel inches toward the living room, his brown shoes clicking on the linoleum.

It is then that a final clue clicks into place.

"Brown shoes!" I shout, as if that is the only proof needed. "Phyllis said someone with brown shoes and a brown suit was yelling at Barb! It was you! You murdered Barb!"

A crazed look comes over Samuel now that he is caught. "Barb wouldn't sell, and I needed the set! It's worth double if I have the set! Do you know how hard it is to find a set? She was being difficult, so I slipped something into her tea."

Hildy howls her heartbreak and runs out of the kitchen, leaving us to deal with the killer.

I snarl at Samuel in time with my dog. "But you left the

second angel on the mantle after you poisoned Barb. Why not just take it then?"

Samuel's voice turns shrill as he points a finger at Cricket. "Because of that monster! She tried to attack me, so I ran out before I could grab the figurine! I had to wait to get back in until someone found her body and dealt with the dog. Barb should have sold them to me!"

Fury paints my vision red as my fist releases its grip on the leash.

I don't think my actions through; I only know that either I will attack this man, or Cricket will have her fair turn at avenging her mommy.

Cricket wastes not a breath as she leaps into action.

Samuel swings his fist and clocks me in the side of my head when he makes a lunge for the living room, and I block his way.

Stars flash stars in my vision. I cry out, but the sound is eclipsed by Samuel's wail when Cricket chomps on his leg with a meaty growl. His briefcase with the papers Hildy was supposed to sign falls to the floor and pops open.

I stumble forward, but there is little muscle to my movements as I try to blink the world into focus.

Jada screams and takes a swing at Samuel, but he manages to dodge her attack. Samuel shoves Jada so hard that she bangs into the wall.

"Jada!" My cry of horror pierces the air.

My scandalized gasp hits the air when a puzzle piece

tumbles out onto the kitchen floor from the spilled briefcase.

It's the missing puzzle piece from the nature scene Barb was putting together in her dining room when Samuel came to call.

Indignation rises in me. I grasp the puzzle piece as if it is all the proof I need to put this lowlife away for good.

This man shoved Jada, who hugs like she was meant to heal broken hearts.

He got my saint of an aunt put in the hotseat, which is a crime in and of itself.

He murdered Barb, who loved Cricket with a tender heart.

Though my gait is wobbly from my throbbing temple, I lunge toward Samuel and knock him backward until he loses his balance and falls to the ground.

I have never been in a fight in my life, but my fist seems to know the dance well enough to make itself useful. "You murdered Barb!" I shout, crashing atop him. I pin him beneath me, punching over and over across his angular face.

Samuel tries to shield himself with his forearms, but I do not relent, nor does Cricket stop gnawing on his ankle.

Samuel tries to fight back. "She wouldn't sell me the angels! I offered her a fair price. Do you know how rare those figurines are?"

My rage only grows, hitting its peak when Cricket lets out a wounded cry after Samuel's food slams into her face.

"Cricket!" Jada cries, adding a second mournful sound that tugs at my heart. "Hold tight, Hannah! The police are on their way!" She raises her phone.

"Don't you hurt my dog!" I scream at the man. No matter what is happening in the room, the fact that Cricket is injured revives my focus and keeps my goal firmly locked in my mind.

Samuel remains pinned in place beneath my weight. I hit him over and over until Deputy Hanson pulls me off my prey however many minutes later. The truth rings through my body until it finally fills the air. "He did it! Samuel killed Barb!" I tell the deputy, unaware when it was that I started crying.

Jada is far more coherent as she regales the officers with the details of the story. "He stole an angel figurine from Barb when she asked him to auction off her things for her move! When she confronted him, he murdered her! Then he waited for the body to be found so Cricket wouldn't attack him again. He knew his company would be able to come in and finish the auction job, and he would be able to have the second figurine for himself."

The nearest officer nods and hoists me off my prey, handing me to a man I recognize. "Samuel Wilton killed Barb!"

The deputy's arms steady me until he hands me off to another officer. Deputy Hanson rolls Samuel over and slaps handcuffs on the criminal. "Samuel Wilton, you're under arrest for the murder of Barbara Reeves."

He continues his memorized speech while the officer guides me out of the house.

Jada scoops up Cricket, trailing behind us. "You did it," Jada congratulates me, her eyes wide with disbelief. "You found Barb's killer. Finally, Emily's name is cleared."

My chest heaves while the mania crests, leaving me shaking and unsteady, even as I plop down on the front lawn once Jada and the officer lower me to sit beside Cricket.

My dog whines, licking my knuckles even though she was kicked in the face, as if my pain is more important than her own. My arms quake as I reach out to her. I fold her into my embrace while she yips and tells me all about the bad man who murdered her beloved mother.

"I know," I tell Cricket. "He won't hurt anyone ever again."

Jada sits beside me, hugging the two of us tight while we tremble. "The police can take it from here."

The officer nods. "You mind if I go back in there to help Hanson?"

Jada nods. "We'll be okay."

When Samuel is escorted out of the house, I angle my body between Jada and the criminal, just in case he somehow springs free from his cuffs and aims his aggression at my friend. Cricket barks until Samuel Wilton is safely in the back of the squad car.

I sag against my new best friend. "Jada, we just caught Barb's killer. Tell me the worst is over."

Jada hugs me tighter. "I think we're owed a peaceful life from here on out. It's the Apple Blossom Bay promise."

I hope that's true, and that no one attacks my sweet dog ever again.

24

THE PLACE FOR STRAYS

I don't know much about hospitality in a small town, but I figure a hug should say whatever a hug is supposed to say in situations like this.

Jada gets an embrace that squeezes Samuel's shove out of her.

Then Phyllis gets a hug when we come home with Cricket, and she is visiting with Aunt Em. After all, Phyllis gave me the clue about the man in the brown suit yelling at Barb before her death. That sealed Samuel as the killer in my mind when push came to shove.

Phyllis' coo of affection goes straight to my heart as she runs her hand over my back and then kisses my cheek before I pull away.

I am new to hugging, after all.

Jada spills the details of the eventful day we've had, and the arrest that will but Barb's murder case to rest. I keep quiet, grateful to have escaped the brawl with a happy ending.

"Oh, girls. I'm so glad you girls are okay." Phyllis hands us matching mugs with hot tea in them. "Extra honey. Just what the doctor calls for when you wrestle a murderer to the ground." Her gown today is bright yellow. It glitters around the hem that brushes the floor. Her puffy sleeves make her look regal.

Or perhaps it's the proper way she holds herself that makes Phyllis look like a queen.

I glance at the table, noting that Em and Phyllis have been working on my puzzle while I was out. I smile at the team effort, grateful I don't get to enjoy the triumph alone.

I sip my tea, checking Cricket's maw over and over to make sure she is okay.

The little scamp couldn't be happier. Phyllis brought her a few pieces of bacon, which she feeds my posing pup in bits.

I keep my eyes on my fingers while I sit with the ladies, pursing my lips when there's a lull in the conversation. "Aunt Em, I have a favor to ask you." I start to squirm because I don't know how to ask for what I want—not when it's something this big. "See, Barb's daughter doesn't want Cricket. She suggested I take her to the pound."

Phyllis and Em gasp in unison, scandalized that anyone might not fall instantly in love with Cricket. Phyllis holds her nose up. "I don't believe it. I refuse. This is the most perfect dog in the world."

Em shakes her head. "Cricket's not going to the pound. I won't stand for it."

I can't find the words, and if I did, I'm not sure I could muster the courage to force them into the air. I meet my aunt's eyes with a pleading that says it all.

If I cannot keep this beautiful dog, I am certain my heart will wither and die.

Em angles her head toward Cricket and lowers her hand for the sweet fluffball to lick. "I think Cricket should stay with us. What do you think, Hannah?"

"Yes!" I cry out, my volume at full blast as my voice cracks with desperation. "Yes, please, Aunt Em! I'll take care of her and make sure she gets walked, bathed, fed, and let out. I'll do it all! Please, let me keep her."

Em's smile assures me that she will not let the spark my heart needs die out and be taken away. She lifts Cricket onto her lap and lets my new dog kiss her face all over. "It looks like Cricket found her way home after all."

Jada kneels beside my beautiful dog. "Hear that, little cutie? You get to stay!"

Cricket yips happily, as if she understands every word.

Phyllis' hand goes over her heart. "This is the perfect place for strays."

Phyllis is not wrong. I feel as if I have been wandering aimlessly through my life until I landed here, in the sweet small town of Apple Blossom Bay.

25

PUZZLING TOGETHER

*T*he next day, I drive to Puzzles and Pins with Cricket in the passenger's seat. Her tongue is out, and I swear, I can tell she is smiling.

With Samuel behind bars, life is a whole lot simpler as I drive through the main street of Apple Blossom Bay. The trees are budding, readying to show off their flowers that announce spring is in full swing.

My hand drifts to Cricket's brownish-blondish-reddish fur, loving the connection that is always there when I need it. "You look happy," I tell her, and she licks my hand to let me know she truly is.

I know the feeling.

When Hildy gave me her blessing to adopt Cricket and located the necessary papers, I hopped online and got Cricket registered to me in as few keystrokes as possible to get the job done. Aside from nursing a tender spot on the side of my head from Samuel's punch, it is the best life I could have possibly imagined. I love driving with my dog in the car, grinning beside me with the windows rolled down.

My dog.

Cricket is dressed in a blue gingham frock with lace around the hem, looking as pretty as any dog could ever be. She yips occasionally at the scenery going by, letting me know that we are two girls who can handle anything if we are together.

When I pull into the parking lot of Puzzles and Pins, I have two puzzles in my hand and Cricket's leash in the crook of my elbow. Vivian hugs me when I walk into her store, and sure enough, she pulls a dog biscuit from her apron.

My goodness, this is a friendly town.

Cricket sits like a good girl, waiting patiently for the treat.

Vivian coos at the cuteness before she leans down and feeds it to Cricket. "I hear you took a bite out of the bad guy for old Barb. Good girl!" She pets my pup and then straightens, brushing her red hair over her shoulder and straightening her nametag. "And I hear we have you and Jada to thank for finding Barb's killer and getting him turned over to the cops."

I nod and hand Vivian the boxes I brought from my car. "This was the last puzzle Barb borrowed, complete with all one-thousand pieces. I thought you might want it back. If she loved puzzles as much as I do, I'm willing to bet she would be salty if this didn't get returned to you."

Vivian claps her hands and holds them over her heart. "Oh, thank you! I didn't think I would see this one again. You truly brought it back here?"

"Now more people can enjoy it."

"Thank you, Hannah!" Vivian greets two women who come in and head to a room at the back of the store that sits between the puzzle side and the sewing section of the store.

I crane my neck curiously. "What's that back there, Vivian? More puzzles?"

Vivian shakes her head. "That's the puzzle room. People meet up to do group puzzling together. It's like a quilting club or a book club, except with puzzles."

My mouth falls open as the world shifts before my very eyes. I had no idea that was a thing people could do here. "People do puzzles together back there? Are you serious?"

Before I know it, a breath of elation hits my system, expanding my chest and alerting me that this is something I should jump on. The last time I had that feeling was mud sledding and volunteering to look after Cricket, and both those things made me feel more alive than I ever have before. I decide to trust my aunt's advice that I should do something good for myself. I take a chance and lean into the urge.

I touch Vivian's wrist. "Could I join a group? Do I need to put my name on a list or something?"

Vivian's arm falls around my shoulders as she walks me to the room in question. "Nope. You just show up and make friends. I'll introduce you to the girls." She brings me to the entryway of a small room that's only a little bigger than Aunt Em's living room. There is a large round table in the center and folding chairs off to the side. "Ladies, this is Hannah, Em's niece. Little girl just in from the big city. She tracked down the last puzzle Barb did and made sure it was returned to us. You got room for another puzzler?"

My veins freeze as nerves take me over. What if they say no? What if they don't want me to join them? They've got a good thing going in here. Why would they want a stranger to come in and ruin things? What if I make a mistake and bend a puzzle piece? What if I knock over the table in a clumsy moment and puzzle pieces go flying?

A little old lady smiles at me. "Of course! I'm Edna, and this is Lorraine. Phyllis is on her way."

My smile brightens. "I've met Phyllis! You sure you wouldn't mind? I've never put a puzzle together in a group before."

Edna waves me to her side. Instead of shaking my hand, she gives me a tight hug with her bony arms. "Of course not. Any puzzler is welcome here. And you brought Cricket? It's like Barb is still here with us. This is the way it should be. Barb used to puzzle with us. It's like Cricket brought us someone to fill her spot so our hearts wouldn't be empty."

It's a grand declaration that I don't take lightly.

Lorraine removes a butterfly broach from her blouse and pins it to my cheap gray t-shirt, suddenly classing up my whole outfit. "We've been horribly sad without Barb. I'm glad she sent us you."

My hand goes over my heart while Cricket sits at my feet, looking up at Edna as if waiting for a treat.

My goodness, we are spoiled.

Phyllis joins the group a minute later with a box tucked under her arm. "Don't start the party without me, girls! I brought snacks." She sets down a container of homemade chocolate chip cookies while Lorraine pops the lid off the nature-themed puzzle. "Oh, good! Hannah's joining us?"

I nod tentatively, but Phyllis' response of applause makes it clear that worry has no place here.

Though I am new to this group (and this seaside small town), there is nowhere I would rather be than working on a puzzle with new friends and my dog by my side.

Maybe I won't drift forever. Maybe I've finally found my place. My people.

My home.

26

THE CLOWN'S ASSISTANT

I look down at my outfit. "I don't know about this," I tell my aunt. "I'm not exactly trained."

Aunt Em snorts at my hesitation. "Neither am I. I learned all I needed to know watching videos on how to tie balloons and make them into animal shapes. Trust me, the kids don't care if you get it perfect; they just want a friend to play with."

Jada grimaces after she drops the juggling balls yet again. "Maybe we should switch, Em. I'm not making much progress learning how to juggle."

"Try eating a donut," Aunt Em suggests. "Benjamin dropped them off for Hannah and you as a reward for helping solve the case. They're on the counter." Her neck shrinks. "What's left of them, anyway. I may have had one."

Cricket yips, then stands up on her hind legs, showing

off her talent to encourage Jada. Her multi-colored skirt flips down, making me want to ditch this slide whistle in my hand so I can spend the afternoon petting her belly.

"We can do this," Jada says to herself and to me.

I frown at Jada as she picks the ball up off the floor. "I don't know what I'm doing. The kids are going to smell the inexperience on me." I motion to Jada's triangle-themed clown costume. "You look fantastic. I look unprofessional."

Jada snorts at my verdict. "You think the problem is whether or not you look professional? Please tell me you've never gone on a job interview dressed like either one of us." She tosses two balls in the air in the center of my aunt's living room, waiting until she finds her rhythm before she adds the third.

I motion to my neon yellow figure-distorting outfit with disdain. "I would never believe I am a clown. The kids are going to see right through me. Aunt Em, you can do balloon animals. Jada, you can juggle. The slide whistle is the best I can do? They're going to be disappointed."

As if on cue, Jada drops one of her balls.

I motion to my form. "All I can do so far is paint myself in clown makeup that you had to fix, Aunt Em, put on silly clothes and blow a whistle. Those are not clown skills."

My Aunt Em doesn't let anything fluster her, and this conundrum is no exception. She waves off my anxiety. "The kids don't care. I'm telling you, after they've had a day of chemo, all they want is for someone to be kind to them. Make them feel human again."

I chew on my lower lip.

Jada stops juggling and stares at me, her head tilted to the side. "You're stressing. Talk to me. What big, scary monster is following you around?"

Jada doesn't ask as if I am ridiculous to worry. She considers my flustered demeanor with the kindness of one who was born to be a kindergarten teacher, filled with compassion.

I shove my hand in my oversized pocket. I try to ignore the itch on the end of my nose, so I don't smear my white grease makeup yet again. "This is way outside of my comfort zone. I want to do a good job for the kids because they deserve my best, but I don't know what my best looks like. There's no manual."

Aunt Em's mouth twitches as if I've said something cute. "I know what you need. Perhaps you'll do better with your emotional support animal."

My eyebrows lift but then my shoulders droop. "They won't let a dog into the hospital. Though, wouldn't that be fun? Talk about giving kids a morale boost. You can't have a bad day if Cricket is in the room. It's physically impossible."

Aunt Em points at the dog who is never more than two feet from my side. "Actually, Barb used to take Cricket to the library so the kids could practice reading to her. She's a certified therapy dog, Hannah. If you want to take her with you to the hospital, you might have to sign a few forms and bring her papers along, but you can absolutely do that."

My posture straightens. "Are you serious? That's an option?"

Aunt Em nods. "Of course. It's Apple Blossom Bay, not the city. We tend to do what works around here, not what's expected. Those kids would be over the moon if you brought in a dog for them to pet. Give it a try. Every clown needs a purpose. Maybe this is yours."

I mull over her words.

Every clown needs a purpose.

That is the thing that's been missing from my life. I've ticked all the boxes, taken all the tests, and done all the tasks expected of me in life, but in the end, I moved away from it all because I felt empty, no matter how many rules I followed.

Sure, a clown needs a gimmick. Aunt Em has balloons. Jada has juggling. Talking to new people used to be a struggle for me, back when I lived in the city. Everything was online, so it was easier not to take chances. I didn't have to be brave—not really. No one noticed or cared that I slowly started fading into the background, then disappeared altogether.

Taking Cricket around the town has given me a streak of boldness I did not know I possessed. I've taken her on walks through an expansive portion of the town, smiling most of the way. Cricket struts, so it reminds me that I have to at least put one foot in front of the other. She makes me braver than I could ever be on my own.

I decide to take my aunt's advice.

"Give me one minute, and we'll be ready to go." Excitement pushes at my worry, making it small enough that a smile finally takes over my face, widening the one I have painted across my cheeks. "Cricket needs a different outfit."

Aunt Em claps while Jada giggles at the sizable stack of dog clothes I took from Barb's house. They were deemed worthless and unsellable, but to me, they are the source of real, priceless joy.

And hopefully, it won't just be me who squeals at the sight of my precious toy Pomeranian dressed up as a hot dog with a French fry hat.

I glance up apologetically at the two who are gushing at the cuteness. "I'll get her a proper clown costume for the next time we do this."

I don't realize what I am saying until the words come out.

I am committing to this odd activity, planning to step outside of my comfort zone again and again. That bravery was not part of my DNA before I came to the sweet little town of Apple Blossom Bay. But now that I am here, cuddling the best dog in the whole world, I begin to believe that this town will accept me, even if I don't have the answers, so long as I take that first step out the front door.

Jada, Aunt Em, and I strut out into the sunshine, following Cricket's lead.

I may not know all there is to understand about life,

but I do know for certain that this world is better with friends, family, and a fluffy dog.

The End

FREE PREVIEW

Enjoy a free preview of the next book
in the Apple Blossom Bay series,
Corgi Crisis.

27

CORGI CRISIS

*W*aking up to my sweet toy Pomeranian laying her head on my stomach is just about the best feeling in the world. Though Cricket is six years old, her squat stature, curious nature and fluffy hair make her look like she is still a pup.

Though my Aunt Em's ranch-style home isn't set directly on the beach, with my window open, I can feel the ocean air wafting in through the gap.

If there is a town, a home, a life more perfect than this, I do not know it.

I sit up slowly and kiss Cricket on her wet nose, letting her listen to my plans for the day while I take my time stroking her thick fur. I can't decide if it's more red, brown, or gold today. Either way, she shines with happiness as I rub the velvet of her ear.

"Today is the day," I tell Cricket, who licks my face over and over.

My gosh, being kissed just for waking up? How did I go my entire life without a dog? While I wish the manner in which she came to me didn't involve her previous owner passing away, I am grateful fate trusts that I will care for this sweet dog.

"Today I'm going to the grocery store to apply for a job." I nuzzle my pup's nose with my own. "Is it a management position? No, it's not." I cup her small face with my left hand. "Is it using my business degree? No, it's not. But let me tell you, I can't imagine I will be stressed out stocking shelves at a grocery store. Aunt Em said I should find something that's good for me. I don't know if stocking shelves is it, but it'll give me a little income while I figure out what it is I'd like to do."

I'm not applying because I think the work will be simple; I think this will be good for me because it's not a job that turns my stomach.

After graduation, I was supposed to go straight into a career using my business degree, but I just couldn't do it. Compliant my whole life to the point of letting my parents pick my degree, I didn't realize how ill-suited I was for my impending profession until I was supposed to go job hunting in my field, and I just couldn't do it.

I ended up working at a gas station for a handful of years, much to the embarrassment of my parents, who constantly remind me that I should do more, have more, be more.

So, my parents sent me to the beachy town of Apple Blossom Bay "to take care of Aunt Em" they promised. Though, when I got here last month, it became clear that my spontaneous and often unconventional aunt needs no help from me whatsoever.

I stand from the spacious queen-sized bed and select my most responsible, no-nonsense ensemble—black pants and a white blouse with black shoes. Can't go wrong. This is my least wrinkly blouse, too, which has to count for something.

I tug my messy strawberry blonde curls into a ponytail, and figure I look as good as I should for a job interview. I straighten my posture, claiming every bit of my five-foot-eleven inches.

Cricket doesn't leave my side, even as I flit through the hallway to the kitchen, where Aunt Em is fiddling with the burner on her purple stove. "Good morning!" she sings to me.

I inhale a deep drag of the spring ocean air that is now combined with the smell of bacon. "Any morning with bacon in it is a good one to me." I sneak a piece off the paper towels, my eyes rolling back as the flavor awakens my palate. "Remind me why I lived anywhere other than with you?"

Aunt Em chortles at the compliment. "Let's chalk it up to insanity." She is wearing a flowing silk dress with no waistline, dotted with large pink orchids on the long sleeves. She looks like a spring fae with her shoulder-length straight black hair swept back from her angular jaw and high cheekbones. She stands two inches taller than me and wears her superior height with the confidence of a supermodel. "Did you sleep okay?" she asks me as she plates a few pieces of bacon, a slice of toast and a fried egg for me.

"I slept great. How do I look?"

"Like you're ready to get any job you go after." She narrows one hazel eye at me in a faux scold. "Though, I told you that you don't have to work, you know. You just moved here last month. You haven't taken barely any time to live and figure out what it is that makes you come alive. I don't want you committing to something that makes you miserable."

Cricket yips twice, taking umbrage with that assessment, as if she is not the creature who has brought color to my cheeks and a pep in my step. As if a job can even compare with the joy she brings me.

I feed her a piece of bacon after filling her dog bowl and getting her clean water, all while mulling over my aunt's words. "I'm okay with acclimating slowly to life in Apple Blossom Bay, but I can work a job while I figure out what makes me come alive. What if the thing that makes me come alive is stealing yachts? I might need to have bail money stashed away, just in case."

Aunt Em laughs at what is clearly the furthest thing

from what I might ever do with my life. I am a rule follower through and through. But sure, in my imaginary life, perhaps I steal boats and race across the coast.

Aunt Em sits with me, her upper lip curling when I take a bite of my toast. "Um, you forgot to put butter on that."

I shrug. "It's fine dry." And that's exactly what it is. *Fine.*

My aunt blanches, though I'm not sure her revulsion is from the dry toast or from the F-word that slipped off my tongue. "Fine? You woke up today, deciding life would be nothing more than 'fine'?" She shakes her head at my inadequate priorities. "That toast needs butter, jam or both."

I smirk at her insistence over things that I'm not sure matter all that much. "I think we're out of the jam Phyllis made. Butter might be nice."

"That's more like it. I don't want you to live like a vagrant." She shakes her head. "Dry toast. I never. It's like I've had no influence on you whatsoever."

I love her insistence over the things that never mattered to me before. Aunt Em is big into the details that make life a luxury, even if they are as insignificant as a pat of butter.

We chat while we eat, which was never the case in my house growing up with my parents. My dad read the paper while my mom scrolled on her phone.

Aunt Em is a treat to eat breakfast beside. She tells me all about the planting she is going to attempt this week, and the family she is taking to look at houses in hopes of selling them the abode of their dreams.

After I kiss her cheek and ready myself to head out the door, I promise Aunt Em that I'll pick up a jar of jam when I'm at the store for my interview.

"Do it, and Phyllis will slap the jar out of your hand. If she comes over and sees store-bought jam in my fridge? I'll never hear the end of it."

I snicker at the mental image of the woman in her seventies growing violent over traitor jam.

I hate leaving Cricket behind, but I'm guessing that's not exactly the move of a professional vying for a job if I take my dog with me on the interview. Though, I'll admit, I am decidedly less confident as I drive down the flower-lined streets in my red sedan toward the grocery store without Cricket by my side.

All through college, I let my introverted nature take over. I don't like to use the term "shut-in," but it might apply in broad strokes. The moment Cricket came into my life, I started to appreciate the fresh air of the great outdoors. The spring weather breathes new life into my bones, reminding me that it's okay I am not a finished product.

"I can do this," I say aloud to myself in my visor mirror as I check to make sure I look professional enough for the interview.

My shoulders sink as I take in my reflection.

I look like a hapless twenty-five-year-old blah. Not a

woman. Not a proud bisexual woman. Not a happy dog-owning woman. A "blah" with frizzy strawberry blonde hair that should be curly, and too many freckles across my nose to count. Why would they hire me? I don't have experience stocking shelves. I ran a cash register at the gas station. I have little frame of reference for what any other job might entail.

Plus, I was born without my right hand. Sometimes people regard me as if I can't do things that people with two hands can do. I don't want the owner of the store to see me as a liability, or worse, a charity case.

The grocery store is open, with a dozen or so customers milling about. The carts are lined up near the entrance, and the woman in her fifties with brightly dyed blonde hair at the cash register waves at me with a big smile.

Because she recognizes me.

Because I live here.

I move toward Betty with what I hope is a smile, but I'm sure my nerves are making me look like I am fending off a grimace. "Morning, Betty. I'm here to meet with Larry for an interview."

She claps for me as if I have already secured the position. Her slender frame bobs up and down excitedly. "That's fantastic, Hannah! Em just texted to let me know you were on your way. She said to tell you you're a shoo-in." She waves me toward the rear of the store. "Larry's in the backroom. Go on through the doors."

My smile turns to a grimace because the interview is minutes away from happening. "Thanks."

Why am I nervous? This isn't my dream job. It's not something that defines whether or not I am a useful person.

Still, my palm is sweating as I head to the back of the store, meandering near the meat section because I am unsure which of the backdoors Larry might be behind. There is also a set of doors to my left, so I'm not totally sure where I should be headed.

I don't just want to walk through, since I see two sets of doors along the back wall. And I'm not an employee, so going into the "Employees Only" area seems like an obvious violation of the rules.

Still, Betty directed me here, so after I look from side to side to make sure no one sees me trespassing, I go into the door at the end of the meat section, hoping this is the correct one.

I tiptoe through the cavernous space. It has flickering lights that make me have to squint so I don't get a headache. The rest of the store meant for customers is well-lit, but this seems to be straight from a horror movie, complete with an echoey quality to my steps and a lingering cold that chills my spine. "Hello?" The cheery bright walls of the grocery store are gone now, replaced with concrete from floor to tall ceiling. I shiver as I crane my neck to see if there is any hint of a person nearby who might direct me to Larry.

I chew on my lower lip as I walk further into wide back area, which is lined with rows and rows of inventory.

I really do love putting things in order. Maybe it won't be the most thrilling job for me to stock shelves, but I enjoy it when items are all aligned.

"Hello? I'm looking for Larry," I call to absolutely no one. My voice sounds timid and there's an A/C unit bellowing to drown out anything short of a shout.

I know this is a small town, but I expect someone to be working back here somewhere.

When I hear a whine, my footsteps pick up, moving me toward the sound. As I go nearer, I notice a tinge of distress, so I trot instead of walk. "Larry?" I call again into the cold, gaping backroom.

When I maneuver around one of the tall shelves stacked with pallets of breakfast cereal, a motion near the ground catches my eye. Though the light is terribly dim as it flickers, I make out what is certainly a dog, whining over a lumpy blanket on the concrete floor.

"Oh, pup! Are you lost?" Though, as I approach the squat corgi, a thrill occurs to me. "Do they allow dogs back here?" I kneel so I can run my fingers over the dog's short caramel-colored fur. Instead of keeping my thoughts to myself, I speak to the dog, who seems in need of a friend. "If I got a job here, would they let me bring Cricket?" Glee lights up my face at the prospect. That would be a dream come true. With my dog by my side, I don't reach for anxiety as often as I normally might. She calms me down and breaks the ice with strangers.

My insides lift with my next inhale—a deep breath that tells me my happiness is buried in that very idea.

The corgi leans into my touch, licking my wrist to let me know she is friendly.

"What are you doing back here all by yourself?" I kiss the top of the corgi's head. "Did someone drop a package, and you're cleaning it up for them? I hope you got to eat something tasty." I pick up the blanket beside her, which has something bumpy underneath.

The corgi whines and then lets out a mournful howl when the blue blanket slips over the secret it was hiding beneath.

I gasp and leap backwards, crying out in terror. My voice echoes through the concrete walls, making it sound like there are several of me calling out for help.

I back up, my eyes fixed on the horror as my mouth refuses to close. I drop the blanket several feet from the gruesome sight, though I probably should have covered it back up for propriety's sake.

The corgi sticks by my ankles, whining because neither of us knows what to do with the dead body of a man, lying abandoned in this cold and lonely space.

Read the next book in the Apple Blossom Bay series today!

PEANUT BUTTER DOG BISCUITS

to help with sore joints

Yield: 20 treats

"After a long day, there is nothing I like more than squishing the biscuit ingredients and turning them into a sticky lump while my problems fade to the background. In fact, the longer I take, the less anxious I become. I am no longer worried that I am taking up space in her home. As Cricket sits at my feet while I knead and push my problems out of the way, I realize that I like it here."

-Pomeranian Puzzle by Molly Maple

Ingredients for Biscuits:
   2¼ cup almond flour

¼ cup ground flax meal

1 egg

1 cup peanut butter

1 cup water

3 Tbsp turmeric

Instructions for Biscuits:

1. Preheat oven to 350 degrees F.
2. Mix with a large spoon the almond flour, ground flax meal and egg in a large bowl until well combined.
3. Add peanut butter, water, and turmeric, mixing until the dough is sticky but holds together in a ball.
4. Refrigerate for one hour.
5. Using a spoon or a melon baller, scoop the cookies in a round shape.
6. Place on a lined baking tray and bake 15-20 minutes. When the kitchen starts to smell like peanut butter cookies, they might be starting to burn, so pull them out and set the pan on a cooling rack immediately.
7. Cool on the tray ten minutes, then transfer to a cooling rack until completely cooled.

Store in an airtight container in the fridge for up to four weeks.

Author Molly Maple believes in the magic of hot tea and the romance of rainy days.

She is a fan of all desserts, but cupcakes have a special place in her heart. Molly spends her days searching for fresh air, and her evenings reading in front of a fireplace.

Molly Maple is a pen name for USA Today bestselling fantasy author Mary E. Twomey, and contemporary romance author Tuesday Embers.

Visit her online at www.MollyMapleMysteries.com. Sign up for her newsletter to be alerted when her next new release is coming.

Made in United States
Orlando, FL
07 June 2022

18583480R00124